GONE TOO FAR WEST

FACTUAL FICTION

ISOBEL WYCHERLEY

ACKNOWLEDGMENTS

Thank you for buying my first novel! A lot of love, sweat and tears went into this one.

The support that I received from day one from family, friends and even strangers is what made me want to achieve this goal even more. My sister, Gud, has been a great wing-woman throughout the process, helping me brainstorm the initial ideas and giving me feedback on what's good and what's not. You couldn't have done more to help me. I wouldn't have been able to do it without you.

And thank you to Lily for drawing the amazing front cover. I know we had a lot more in store for this one but the cover couldn't be better and hopefully there'll be plenty more times we can collaborate again.

Lastly, thank you to everyone who features in this

book (though you might not thank me). Although loosely based, you made 2018 as west and amazing as it really was. So, here's my gift to you, all those memories written down in a book.

I hope you enjoy reading *Gone Too Far West* as much as I enjoyed writing it and I hope you aren't too offended by your character! Thank you all. So much, peace and love to ya x

INTRODUCTION

Lazy, unorganised, unmotivated, unemployed, and uneducated. But I'm not 'un' anything. I go to college every week, I have a good part-time job and I'm no lazier than your average eighteen-year-old. I guess you could say I'm not your typical stoner.

My name is Felicity, Flic for short. I live at home with my parents, Stuart and Amanda, and my older sister, Laurie. My mum is very anti-drugs, has never taken any herself and she's not afraid to tell you that. She's a small woman with short, dark hair, a pretty face and the smoothest skin you've ever seen. She doesn't shy away from confronting anybody when she thinks they've done wrong. And then there's my dad. He's one of the most interesting people I've ever met, everyone loves hearing stories from his past. Like our Mandy, he's never really been into drugs, he says, but there is one story that slips out every time he's drunk, about his best friend presenting a bag of weed at my parents' housewarming party with the words: "Evening, gentlemen."

My dad is tall and in good shape, despite his gammy knees, elbows, feet and back...

He's open to drug humour, always asking if I want any 'devil's lettuce' on my burger. Despite this, he'd give me a swift left hook to the throat if he found out just how much I craved a drag of the real devil's lettuce.

And last but not least, there's Laurie. We're closer than any sisters in the world. Why? Because we have the same sense of humour, similar interests, the same parents, and a love for all things that get you high.

Our favourite band is Tenacious Toes, an Australian group who, for me, personify everything that is nice about life; summer, love and times spent lazing around with your friends. And I'm lucky enough to be flying over to the weed capital of the world soon, where the grass is always greener, to watch them perform live. AMSTERDAM. I'll be living every stoner's dream.

Laurie looks completely different to me. Sometimes we even question whether we really are related or not. I'm small, with brightly coloured hair, skinny limbs, and attached to my face are numerous nose rings, which my grandma hates, and a pair of black, round spectacles. Laurie is taller, with long, brown hair and bright blue eyes, plus a single nose stud, which our grandma apparently loves. Wonder who's her favourite?

We spend a lot of time together, going to the pub, playing pool, or smoking weed. No matter what we do, we do it crying with laughter.

As much as I love my sister, however, I spend most of my time with my three best friends: Jenk, Len and Javan. You will find us in our favourite spot in Paradox Park, on a big picnic bench that's covered in the carvings and graffiti of other stoners who use this bench as their haven. The bench is situated with a vast forest behind it, which goes on for miles, and a large stretch of grass in front, which connects you to the car park and the entrance, so you really feel out in the open, vulnerable, like it's just us four against the world, we've only got each other.

Jenkies, once a shy boy I never spoke to in high school, is now the guy who provides the drugs for our little rendezvous in the park. He is very tall, almost too tall, and lanky as anything. He has shoulder-length blond hair that curls around at the ends, and which is usually sticking out from beneath his lucky bucket hat, red with navy blue flowers sprawled unsymmetrically around it. Your typical stoner, he stays away from confrontation and makes it very hard for anyone to dislike him, with his catchphrase being "finesse, never stress."

Len, on the other hand, is quite the opposite. He's always been very confident and self-assured, one of those 'I'm the best-looking person in this room' types of people, despite him also being a nervous wreck. Upon his head sits short, blond, curly hair and his face is always plastered with a perfect white grin. He has broad shoulders and a good swimmer's back, all topped off with the most chiseled six-pack you've ever seen. Everybody knows his name, and he's aware of it. But despite this, he isn't as arrogant as you would expect. He's actually more like a giant child, always laughing and telling jokes. He doesn't take himself too seriously, somehow.

And finally, there's Javan. He too is very tall; slightly smaller than Jenk, though. His big, sunken eyes are almost covered behind his long, brown, unkempt fringe. The poor boy hasn't been given the best chances in life. He can't seem to stay in college for long or hold down a weekend job for more than two months, meaning he never has any money to afford the drugs, and he still owes us all money from last month, too. Because of this hardship, he's become very depressed, but there are some lengths he goes to that we didn't even know about. But, similar to Len, he knows how to take a joke, and for a moment he forgets about the difficulties he faces and enjoys the time we spend together.

When I'm not out enjoying myself, I'm either in college or at work. All my friends go to the same college as me, but we're not in any lessons together, apart from me and Jenk getting a few cherished hours in our media lessons, but our breaks are always spent together as a group. I also study drama, English language, and Extended Project Qualification. For those of you that don't know what EPQ is, it's a trap they lure you into by saying it will help you get into your chosen university, when all it does is diminish your will to live. For this subject, you are told to write a dissertation, and deliver a PowerPoint presentation to the class. The topic of this is down to you. I chose to write about the effects of different drugs on the mind and the body, where as other students chose things like 'Is there such a thing as a sustainable city?' or stuff about Shakespeare, so it's safe to say that my project sticks out like a lazy, unorganised, unmotivated, drug-fuelled thumb.

I work weekends behind the bar in a local pub. It's full of creepy old men who ask me out on dates or ask where I live. But overall, I suppose I do enjoy working there. A job's a job, as they say, and this job pays for me to get high, so I can't complain.

Already, this year has been the best of my life. We've had the hottest summer Britain has seen in years, I met my favourite band in my new favourite city and, most surprisingly of all, the England team were flying through the World Cup. Morale and patriotism were at an all-time high, just what we needed.

Except, after falling ill on holiday, doctors gave me one last feeble year to live and I wanted to make the most of it. But little did I know that something would happen that would test the foundation of every relationship I have and put a strain on the lives of everybody involved. Stories came out in the news, but nobody knows what really happened. I'm the only person who can tell you all. The true story needs to finally be told.

ONE MONTH BEFORE:
SERVICE WITH AN UPSIDE-DOWN SMILE.

To start off the summer, my family always have a holiday to somewhere hot, Menorca being the destination for this year. We get to the airport at five a.m. We're all tired and very quiet, asking each other if we're excited for the holiday in the most unenthusiastic voices ever.

The flight is over quickly. Everybody is asleep as I watch a couple of episodes of a series Jenk had told me to watch and by that time, we're landing.

Once we're in Menorca airport, my dad goes to find the taxi company that's supposed to be driving us to our villa. He returns with a man who looks more like an ex Spanish wrestler than a taxi driver. He's massive, and he has a dark handlebar moustache, receding black hair and olive skin. You can also see his pristine white vest top under his thin, white collar shirt with the first few buttons undone, displaying a jungle of curly, black chest hair and a big gold chain.

He snatches the suitcase in front of me, in the urgent Spanish manner that most natives have, and he leads us to the minibus.

Only, it isn't a minibus; in fact, you could say it is quite the opposite. I stand watching Padre Loco load our suitcases onto an empty double-decker bus.

"Go on then, get on," Dad says, with a smirk appearing on his face.

I get on the bus and I almost start to walk up the stairs to sit on the top deck, as if it's the school bus, but instead I perch down on a set of four chairs surrounding a little plastic table. Laurie and mum join me there too.

"What the hell?" Mum whispers as she sits down next to me.

Dad steps onto the bus as Luchador El Diablo finishes putting our suitcases in the luggage hold, on the outside of the bus. He sits on his own on the opposite table to ours.

"Might as well spread out," he jokes, as he breathes in awkwardly through his teeth, which makes us all laugh.

"Did you know it was going to be a double-decker bus?" I whisper, as El Generico bumbles onto the bus and crashes into the driver's seat.

Dad shakes his head and laughs.

The bus journey isn't as long as I expect it to be. Within forty-five minutes we are picking up the keys to our new casa for the week.

We get off the bus and El Mysterio passes us our cases back without a smile in sight.

"*Gracias!*" I chirp, in my best Spanish accent which I picked up from one year of A-level Spanish, which I then failed and dropped out of. He just nods back at me with his upside-down smile.

The villa's your typical casa: white walls, tiled floors, orange roof and outdated, wooden furniture. We get changed into more appropriate clothes and chill out in the high temperatures. The scene is bliss. I'm floating around in the pool on my back, looking up at the beautiful, clear, blue sky, the giant orange sun tanning my pale, white skin and warming up the pool to the most perfect temperature. My dad is lying on his back on a sunbed in the shade, reading his book peacefully, whilst Laurie and mum sunbathe in the pool, clinging to the side, stretching their legs out in front of them. All I can hear between the dull droning of the filter underneath the water is the sound of tweeting, coming from the tiny brown birds wandering around the poolside, pecking at anything they find on the floor. I close my eyes as I think to myself, *this is the most peaceful and relaxed I've ever been...* and I float my hands through the clear water, breaking through the still hotness of it, blessing my skin with a much cooler covering than before.

As we've been rushing around, unpacking and sorting everything out around the villa, we were too busy to notice the family also moving in to the villa next door to ours. Living there for the next week would be a father and a mother, a grandmother and two young kids, Isaac and Ellamae. We hear the two kids running outside screaming as they're finally let loose to explore their new surroundings.

But their dad will not be allowing that. "No. No. You come here, Isaac. Only one of you in the pool at a time. Get your armbands on. I can't look after both of you at the same time. ELLAMAE!"

I lift my head out of the water and turn around to look at my mum and Laurie. They're already looking at my dad, and he's looking at me. We pull concerned faces at each other – apart from my mum, who's rolling her eyes and looks like she'd rather be anywhere else but our own private paradise.

Then, the loud, arrogant father starts to try and teach the little boy how to swim,

"Go on, kick your legs! It's not all about strength, Isaac, it's all about technique! If we keep practising like this every day, your technique will get better and you'll get stronger as well! ELLAMAE, GET OUT

OF THE POOL! ONLY ONE AT A TIME IN THE POOL!"

However, Isaac isn't listening to his dad's elite Olympic training and Ellamae isn't listening to her dad's annoying outbursts of anger. And, unsurprisingly, we don't want to listen to it, either, so we walk into town with only one thing in mind, a full English breakfast.

We walk past rows and rows of cafés and restaurants, but none of them are offering us exactly what we want. After what seems like forever in the sweltering heat, we finally find a British bar that advertises a full English, with hash browns included. Dad tries to kid himself with thinking that we might find an even better place to eat, so we continue to walk down the road for a while until I order, rather than ask, "Shall we turn back and go in there now?"

To which everybody instantly replies, "Yep." And we march back to the trusty British bar.

The owner is a middle-aged cockney man named Mark. He comes over and takes our order and chats about the England-versus-Columbia game that's on tonight, which, if we win, will catapult us into the quarter finals. When the breakfast arrives, it is unbelievable. Everything you could possibly desire was piled up on the plate: sausage, bacon, baked beans, fried egg, toast, hash browns, mushrooms,

5

black pudding – perfect! I sit there, too busy eating to join in with the conversation about returning later that night to watch the England game here, but I agree more than ever that we should definitely return; perhaps tomorrow lunchtime as well.

After we finish our delicious feast, we walk back to the villa and cool down from the long, hot walk by jumping into the refreshingly cold pool. For the rest of the day, the only thing me and dad talk about is how good the breakfast was, which then brings us onto the subject of barbecues. Even just saying the word 'barbecue' brings a shimmer of light to my dad's eyes, like a kid in a sweet shop. He excitedly decides to walk down to the supermarket to buy all the barbecue essentials with Mum, and that's exactly what they do. I settle down on the green, almost sagging with age, sofa, next to the one that Laurie is on whilst playing a game on her phone.

"Have Mum and Dad gone out?" she asks.

"Yeah, they've gone to the supermarket," I reply.

"Fancy a spliff?" she inquires, without taking her eyes away from her phone.

I don't bother to question her on how she has this weed, I think I'd rather not know, in fact.

We sit outside on a sunbed in the middle of the grassy area and spark up the spliff. We decide to smoke it as quick as humanly possible to make sure we don't get caught by anybody.

I have my last drag and sit on the end of the

sunbed with my eyes closed and my face tilted up to the sun, Laurie finishing the spliff next to me. I start to feel it more, rising inside of me. The world booms methodically in my ears as if it has its own pulse and I can feel tiny beads of sweat dripping from my hairline. My jaw starts clenching due to the very strange feeling in my teeth and I start to take deep breaths in order to try and be relaxed.

"Are you okay?" Laurie asks, concernedly.

"Yeah!" I quip, thinking I have it in me to pretend like my whole body isn't melting into a puddle on the floor.

"Flic... I'm going to ask you one more time... Are you okay?"

"...NEED SHADE."

I run over to the other side of the pool where the shadow of the sun behind the villa shelters a set of sofas outside. I lie down and close my eyes. Being on a harder surface makes me feel a whole lot better since I know I'm stuck to the ground and not going anywhere, and so my head and my heart begin to settle again. I take a deep breath as the cold breeze washes over my face, instantly relieving me.

I sit up and look at Laurie, who's now laughing and walking over to me.

"That was so scary, but so funny," she laughs, as she sits down on a chair next to the sofa

"Thought I was going to die, ha-ha." But the

laugh portrays itself as slightly more feeble than I anticipated.

After deciding that I'll never take drugs in a hot country ever again, we go back inside to pretend as if nothing had happened. Mum and Dad return with multiple shopping bags full of food and alcohol and they couldn't look more excited about it.

Dad goes straight to the little stone barbecue in the corner of the garden and he starts to set up. I sit back on the sofa that I previously nearly died on and look out into the garden. The beautiful, clear blue skies and the equally clear blue pool water both fight for our attention, competing with each other as to which is the bluest, which is the most beautiful. I can't decide; they're both as endearing as each other.

We all sit round the outside dining table and chow down on one of the finest barbecues I've ever had. After that, we all relax a little bit more before getting a shower and getting dressed ready for the World Cup match.

Laurie and I walk ahead of our parents and we laugh about the near-death experience that I had today.

"I honestly didn't know what to do, I thought you were dying."

"Well, thankfully I didn't, as that would have been hard to explain to Mum and Dad." I laugh.

Too busy being immersed in conversation, we don't notice that we've walked directly into the middle of a roundabout with multiple cars approaching

"Nearly dying has made me so hungry. I wonder what we're having for dinn-oh-my-God-we're-in-the-middle-of-a-roundabout!" I shout, with my words stringing together towards the end of my proclamation.

We both laugh in fear, confusion, humour and multiple other nouns as we stand on the grassy island waiting for the cars to pass by.

Finally, our parents catch up to us and they look at their two adult daughters stranded on a roundabout island of disappointment. I shout over for help with a feeble voice crack for added comedic effect, and it works because Dad shakes his head and laughs at the floor.

We decide to eat dinner in the small Italian restaurant directly next door to the British bar before the game starts. It's empty apart from one other English family on a long table at the other end of the restaurant. The waiter comes to the table to take our drinks order. Dad asks for a small beer, Mum sticks with her trusty Bacardi and Coke, and I with my Malibu and Coke, and Laurie attempts to order a Tequila Sunrise, except the waiter doesn't speak English and just decides to reply with a nod and ignores her order.

Three drinks arrive on a silver tray carried by the

same waiter, a small, skinny boy with one of those upside-down smiles.

"Excuse me, we ordered a Tequila Sunrise as well, mate, could you bring it over?"

He just looks at Dad and blinks a few times before whispering, "Mmyes" and walking away slowly to speak to an older member of staff behind the bar.

"Who's Chuckles? Has he ever heard of service with a smile?" Dad spits in irritancy.

"He was smiling, Dad, just the wrong way around," I explain

The older waitress comes over to the table and asks Laurie to point out the drink on the restaurant's menu, which she does. The waitress reads the menu and instantly realises what it is she's asking for,

"OHHHH! Ha-ha, *si, si,*" she laughs, before rushing back to the bar to mix the cocktail.

We finally get the drink and plenty more where that came from.

I get up and order us four caramel vodka shots at the bar, and she looks at me like I'm crazy.

"Caramel vodka," I repeat.

"*Eh?*" she shrieks.

I point to the bottle of caramel vodka behind her. She rotates her head ninety degrees and turns back with a big smile on her face.

"Aah, *vodka caramela!*" She laughs, rolling her

eyes and hitting me on the arm like I was being an idiot.

"Ha-ha... Yeah," I mutter, with a pathetic smile.

Once the football starts, we move across to join the rest of the rowdy English crowd.

If we beat Columbia, it hurtles us into the quarter finals, so the atmosphere is extremely tense once the game ends 1-1, taking us to penalties.

Dad and I stand up at the back of the outside terrace, shoulder to shoulder in a sea of England shirts and red and white face paint. I look around and see people cowering behind their hands as they can't bear to watch.

First to take a penalty is Radamel Falcao, with Jordan Pickford in net. He scores with ease and the crowd seem to lose all hope for a split second. First to take a penalty for England is Harry Kane, the hero of the competition so far.

"There's no way Kane's missing this!" a lad next to me says to his dad, whilst they are both walking up and down the terrace in panic and anxiety.

Thankfully, he doesn't miss, and he smashes it into the bottom left corner of the goal and the whole bar goes insane, including the staff. But it's short-lived, as Johan Mojica takes Columbia's second penalty and it soars right into the top corner. Marcus Rashford steps up to the mark and Dad says something to me about being doomed, but I'm not listening, I'm too engrossed in the tension unfolding on the screen in front of us. He teases us all by side-stepping past the ball before approaching it, the ball flying in a similar way to Kane's penalty. The keeper was very close to making contact with the ball, but he doesn't quite get there, and the crowd cheers again, jumping around and grabbing on to anybody close enough for us to reach.

The next Columbian player scores his penalty, creating an atmosphere so full of tension that you could cut it with a spoon. Next up for England is Liverpool player Jordan Henderson, who Dad and I know all too well. We both voice our displeasure to each other, and some members of the crowd have similar reactions. The keeper reads his movements and jumps and saves the shot. My heart sinks to my stomach and I rest my hands on the back of my head.

"It's all over," one man whimpers, but everybody is thinking it.

There's no hope for anybody at this point. Our stiff stances become more relaxed as we deal with the idea of losing the penalty shootout. But the dismay is short-lived as Pickford saves the next shot, and again, the crowd livens up and the man next to me throws me up in the air and once I land back on the floor, I grab hold of my dad and hug him as he punches the air and jumps around. The next Columbian player misses, and the crowd settles down from another emotional outburst to watch the final England player take his shot. If he scores, England are in the World Cup quarter finals.

I close my eyes for a moment and pray that he scores, we need all the help we can get. Like an old Western film, the two footballers stand opposite to each other, trying to intimidate one another. He takes a few slow steps towards the ball and it travels straight into the bottom left corner, with the keeper nowhere near reaching it.

The crowd explodes into a rage of cheering, screaming, singing and crying as *It's Coming Home* starts to blare out of the surrounding speakers. I can't remember the last time I've felt this relieved and emotional and I'm sure everybody else feels a similar way. We walk back to the table to join Mum and Laurie and we all talk about how exciting the whole experience was and we have a few more drinks.

At around eleven o'clock, Mum and Dad decide to go back to the villa, but Laurie and I decide to stay out for a little while, to celebrate, of course.

The music is still blaring in the bar, but the crowd has thinned considerably. I sit at a small round table whilst Laurie gets the drinks in.

I stare around the bar, looking at the different types of people here and wonder what they're feeling right now. A girl around my age catches my eye. She's sitting at a table on her own, just as I am, except her slightly drunken mother comes over and tries to get her to dance, grabbing her by the wrists and throwing her arms around above her head. I laugh, and she looks over and rolls her eyes, laughing as well. Once her mum leaves her to it, she walks over to me.

"Fancy comin' for a fag?" She leans on the back of the chair in front of me, and she asks in what I would describe as a very strong Essex accent.

I can't leave Laurie here without telling her where I've gone, plus I wouldn't want to miss out on a free drink.

"Yeah sure, why don't you sit down for a minute? My sister's just getting some drinks," I propose, and she takes me up on my offer.

"I'm Carly." She introduces herself, with her southern accent elongating every syllable.

"Nice to meet you, I'm Flic. And this is my older sister, Laurie." I point to her as she sets two strawberry daquiris and two baby Guinness shots down on the table.

They both say "Hi" and Carly reintroduces herself to Laurie.

We talk for a while. Carly tells us how she's been here for months, working in an Indian restaurant, and her sister works here in the bar. She also tells us about a Spanish guy she's invited out tonight. He works on the beach and she met him through friends,

"Yeahhh, it's really awkwaaard, I didn't think he'd actually come!" She laughs shyly.

"Well, we're pretty pissed so we will make it less awkward!" Laurie tries to reassure her.

"Or make it even more awkward," I add, to which we all laugh and agree.

His ears must have been burning because he steps out onto the terrace just as we finish talking about him. He gives Carly a hug and waves at me and Laurie, introducing himself as "Juan."

We tell him to pull up a chair, which he does. We sit there all night, drinking, laughing and telling each other our personal stories as if we'd all been friends for years.

Carly makes a few jokes about lesbians and gays, obviously not realizing that Laurie is a lesbian. We laugh at her jokes and make sly eye contact with each other, which makes us chuckle even more, like naughty school children.

Juan tells us about how he found out his brother was gay. "I was visitin' him, in a place no far from Manchester, where he live. Ehhh... Bolton!" he recalls. "He was in the kitchen, cooking, and he would be dancing to the songs of pepul like, ehhhh, Kati Perri y Ladi Gaga."

Carly turns to me. "KATI PERRI! Hahaha!" she howls. I laugh, with intervals of shushing her as she begins to laugh harder. Thankfully, Juan doesn't know why we're laughing, and we don't tell him. I change the subject by asking him what his brother's name is.

"Pepe," he utters, in his heavy Spanish accent.

Immediately, Laurie starts to laugh. "I could have

guessed that! Ha-ha, that's the two most Spanish names ever! Juan and Pepe!" she manages to gasp, through breathless laughs.

We all start to laugh, even Juan, going as far as to agree with her as well.

"I like your shit shirt by the way, where did you get it?" Carly beckons to Laurie.

"Well, do you like it, or is it shit?" Laurie laughs.

"Nah, you know what I mean. It's called a shit shirt, but some shit shirts are nice," she explains.

"Wouldn't you just call that a nice shirt?" I chip in, confused.

She digs a hole even deeper by calling them lesbian shit shirts, but that only makes us laugh more.

It's coming to around 3 am now and the party is starting to thin. Carly's mother approaches the table and starts to talk to us.

"Have you all had a good night?" she asks, slightly slurred, in that drunken mum sort of way.

"Yeah, it's been good, thanks," or something along those lines, is muttered by all of us, with big, drunken smiles plastered on our little happy faces.

After a few moments of chatting to us, it becomes obvious that Carly's mum is starting to embarrass her. She starts trying to get her to go away, making me concerned about whether an argument will break out at some point. The atmosphere becomes a little bit tense when the comments starting to get slightly bitchy.

"Don't talk to me like that, I'm your mother!" she demands, but not in a negative tone.

And if I were to think of one response that is perfect to that statement, it's the one that Carly surprised us all with. In her slightly moronic, Essex accent she replies, "I knaw, Mam, I came out ya vaginah."

The laughter spits out of our mouths with force as the scene finishes with the dropping of her mother's jaw in astonishment.

It feels like we laughed for hours, but it was probably only around fifteen minutes. Which, if you think about it, is still a long time to be laughing for. It's safe to say that I've never before laughed so much with complete strangers.

As four o'clock comes around, we decide to head back to the villa. We say goodbye to our new acquaintances and start on the long walk back home. The sky is getting brighter, remnants of the dark night sky slowly fading away, allowing the sun's rays to rise into sight. The road we're walking along is long and straight, the pavement is the classic pinkish-red rectangle tiles, which runs alongside a patch of giant mangroves. Rows of quaint little villas, which look like something you'd see in a pirate film, sit peacefully on the other side of the road.

In the distance, I see the Little Red Land Train

that drives eager tourists around the town for a little bit of sightseeing.

"Do you reckon it's unlocked?" I ask Laurie, prompting her to think on the same wave length as me.

She smirks. "Maybe."

I walk up to the first carriage of the train and pull the small silver handle down. I tug on the door and it opens with no force needed. I get Laurie to take a picture of me inside the train. I clamber in and close myself in. I pop my head out of the small, windowless opening in the centre of the door and pull the 'upside-down smile' face.

"I'll take one of you now!" I pronounce excitedly, and we swap places. She climbs into the carriage as I stand on the pavement, camera in hand.

In Laurie's picture, she sits with her body facing forward and her head turned to face the camera. A casual, dumb smile and hardly open eyes is the look she's decided to go for.

I take the picture, trying to hold it steady over my laughter and swaying.

"Let's both get in now," I pronounce yet again. I sit a few rows behind Laurie and pose for the picture. We laugh again, before getting out and continuing our walk.

It only takes around ten minutes for us to find something new to mess around with. A giant inflatable swan, sitting in the front garden of one of the villas on the street.

"Take a picture with that!" Laurie laughs, getting into the spirit of things now.

We both take turns to sit on the swan, which was unfortunate since the sprinklers had been on not long before we showed up. Although I must admit the feeling of the cold water on my skin woke me up slightly. We try and silence our laughter, so as not to wake up the owners of the swan that we're currently sat on, taking pictures with. After we'd taken the pictures, we continue our walk. I walk on ahead, playing on my phone and trying to concentrate on walking straight, and Laurie trails behind me. It doesn't take long for me to notice the constant scraping sound that's followed us during the five-minute journey all the way up the hill and around to the street that our villa is situated on. I turn around and see Laurie laughing and dragging the giant inflatable swan behind her. I'm definitely not in the frame of mind to be serious about this situation, and so I laugh it off and carry on as normal. We get home and Laurie flings the swan into the pool and follows me inside, where we go straight to our room and go to sleep.

The next morning, I wake up and the room is spinning. Laurie is still asleep next to me and I start to panic about the feeling of vertigo. I try drinking some water, but it doesn't make any difference. I close my eyes and manage to hold off the inevitable for around half an hour before I can't anymore. I need to be sick.

I get out of bed and just as I walk past the archway leading to the open-plan living room, Mum turns around and spots me. I smile at her, but just as I do, I gag as well, bringing my hand up to my mouth and heeling over slightly, before I dash off into the bathroom to throw up. Once I've finished, I slump down on the big sofa in the front room and Mum passes me a bottle of water.

"What time did you get in last night?" she queries.

"About half four, I think," I reply, genuinely not sure whether that was the correct time or not.

"That explains it," she says, raising her eyebrows at me and turning away.

But this doesn't feel like a hangover. The room isn't spinning anymore, my stomach isn't unsettled, I just can't stop throwing up. My whole body is aching with fatigue, my eyes start to sting and water as I feel my face heating up. I stand up to put the air conditioning on, but before I get there, I desperately need to stop off at the bathroom again first.

Whilst everyone else is deciding what they're going to do for lunch, I'd rather be thinking about anything other than food. What I choose to think about is my friends back home (mostly Len) and how excited I am about the summer holidays. I think back to that day in college a mere few weeks ago; Jenk and I are sitting on a small playground in the middle of a housing estate that looks like something out of a classy, American, family-friendly film and we're talking about Tenacious Toes and their current world tour.

"They're going to be in London in July, we could go and see them!" Jenk raves and passes me his phone so I can look at the list of dates and countries.

"Or... we could go and see them in Amsterdam. It'd be the same price to fly there as it would to get the train to London... But it'd be more fun in Amsterdam." I smirk, raising an eyebrow in an attempt to make him agree with my idea.

He thinks about it momentarily, then: "I'll put it in the group chat when we get back to college."

"Yes!" I shout, raising my arms in the air. "This is going to be so good, Jenk. Oh my God, I can't wait already!"

"We've not made a decision yet, Flic," he cuts in.

"We're going, Jenk. It has to happen," I insist

And a few days later, our flights to Amsterdam were booked and our gig tickets were ready to print.

But this beautiful memory is interrupted by my dad entering the room and telling me that they're going

21

out for lunch in town and asking if I'd like to go with them. I decline, not feeling well or hungry enough to go. I say goodbye to them all and watch them leave through the little front gate, before lying back down on the sofa and staring at the ceiling.

An hour or so passes and I'm still in the same position as before. My stomach starts to rumble now, and I decide it's probably best if I eat. I walk over to the kitchen and put a piece of bread in the toaster. After sliding down the handle and watching the inside of the toaster start to glow, I lean back onto the worktop and take a few deep breaths. But it doesn't help, because instantly I feel a rush of shivers all over my body. I know what that feeling is. I walk straight to the bathroom, leaving the toast to pop out on its own when it's ready. I have just enough time to tie my hair back before I start to throw up again. Since I haven't eaten all day there is nothing for me to throw up and my throat becomes sore and raw with pain.

This whole saga is abruptly disrupted by the sound of an alarm from right outside the door.

I manage to stop throwing up for a moment. I wash my hands and wipe my face and dash out of the door. The open-plan kitchen/living room is filled with thick grey smoke. For a second, I think the villa is on fire somewhere, until I remember the toast. I run over to the kitchen and see the smoke pouring out of the top of the toaster. I switch it off at the wall and a charcoal piece of toast flies out and smacks down onto the worktop. I grab a newspaper and start to wave it underneath the alarm and it finally goes off, after around twenty seconds of frantically waving the paper around my head.

I open the kitchen window and walk back to the bathroom to continue where I left off. Again, I lean over the toilet and start to throw up nothing. Unbelievably, the fucking smoke alarm sets off again and I have to stop midway to go back into the kitchen and swing the newspaper around my head again! But thankfully, that's the last time it goes off and I collapse back onto the sofa once I finish up in the bathroom.

Not long after, the family return home.

"Has something been burning?" Dad asks.

For the rest of the holiday, I continue to throw up or constantly hold it back, but that doesn't stop me from enjoying the time with my family. We are floating around in the pool as Dad swims lengths, listening to the obnoxious father staying next door and laughing at the things he says.

"Have you ever heard Dad say 'Oh Gyod'? He says it all the time!" I laugh as I tell Mum and Laurie, "I was telling him a dark joke the other day and he said it. Clearly, he didn't find it funny."

"I've heard it before!" Laurie confirms, almost crying from laughter at the sheer memory of it.

Dad decides to get out at the side of the pool to sunbathe and dry off. As he pushes himself out of the pool, water pours out of the little hole on the back pocket of his swimming trunks.

"Dad, did you just wee in the pool?" Laurie jokes, to which he laughs and says, "No!"

"Looks like a whale's blow 'ole, BRR!" Mum shouts, pretending to throw up at the end of her sentence,

"Oh Gyod, Mandy!" he replies, pulling a disgusted face at her as he walks around the pool.

This triggers a series of "OH GYOD!" from Mum, Laurie and I as we all almost drown from laughing too much. Dad just shakes his head and tries not to laugh.

Back home in England, my condition isn't any better; in fact, it has since gotten worse as I am rapidly losing weight due to loss of appetite and not being able to keep anything down. I make an appointment with my doctor and as I sit in the waiting room, I can't help but wonder what some of the possibilities are. Is it just a stomach bug? Food poisoning? I suppose that's what I'm here to find out.

I'm called into his room where he then asks me a few questions about how I feel, and he then proceeds to take tests and examine me. I return later in the week to find out my results. As I sit down in the crooked wooden chair across from him, he intertwines his fingers together on top of his desk. I look at them and acknowledge my own sweaty, trembling hands.

"This is going to be hard for you to hear..." he begins.

And so, this is my final year on Earth. Better make it a good one.

TEN DAYS BEFORE:

BLACK BEAUTY'S ADVENTURE

T he summer term, and exam week specifically, is
well underway at college now. My alarm is set
for eight o'clock, just enough time to get ready and
get to college for half past nine.

As I roll over onto my back after turning off my
alarm, I look around my room to ease me into my
sleepy morning routine. My eyes scan over the
hundreds of pictures covering my walls, lingering
over my favourite one of me and Laurie, when we
were younger. I was just a baby when the picture was
taken, but Laurie still has a protective, older sister
arm resting gently over my tiny body. Looking at it
makes me smile, with the smugness of having the best
sister in the world. Seeing all these pictures of my
loved ones makes me really appreciate how important

it is to make the most of your life, which is exactly what I plan on doing.

As I look over at the window, shielded behind the new, white drawstring blinds, I see the sunshine pouring out of the sides, which puts me in the mood to get ready and enjoy the drive to college. I swing open my wardrobe doors and ponder over which one of my many colourful shirts I'll wear today. I decide on a very sensible Hawaiian shirt, bright red, covered with big blue and green leaves, closed together with little brown wooden buttons. I match this with a pair of blue jeans, which have more holes in them than actual fabric. I do everything else I need to do before heading downstairs.

My dad is sat at his desk, facing away from the door.

"Alright, Flic?"

"I sure am on this glorious summer's morning, Father. How are you?" I sing in my cheeriest voice, this chipper mood being a genuine feeling.

"Alright."

That seems to be as much as I'll get from him this morning, and it speaks volumes, so I make the smart decision of avoiding him until he decides to cheer up. When that will be, I will never know. I walk outside and I get into my car, Black Beauty, start the engine and connect my phone to the speakers. Of course, I put on my Tenacious Toes playlist. I roll down the window and reverse out of the drive.

Waiting at the front of the queue at a set of traffic lights in the centre of town, the sun starts to warm up my car to the perfect temperature and I feel the heat of it on my skin, cooled down every so often by the light breeze coming in through the window. The Hawaiian guitar solo of the TT song kicks in on full volume. I close my eyes and take a deep breath as I revel in this moment of pure bliss.

I sit there for a moment, relaxed and enjoying life.

Until I'm rudely interrupted by the sound of car horns, and an angry male voice.

"Get a move on!" I hear being shouted out of the window of the car behind me.

The light is on green.

I take off my handbrake and start to pull away. I raise my hand to signal 'sorry' to the man who shouted. As I get further away, a few of my outstretched fingers start to bend, leaving only my middle finger stood to attention. How rude.

"Oi!" I hear him spluttering through the mouthful of fumes he just swallowed from the burning rubber of my tyres.

I can't help but laugh to myself as I create more and more distance between me and the man, who now seems to have an axe to grind with me.

I soon stop laughing when I approach the next set of lights. On red.

For a second, I contemplate whether I should just

drive through the crossing traffic, 007 style, but I conclude that I'd rather not die today, so I come to a weary stop and put on my handbrake again. I look into my rearview mirror and I see the man getting out of his car.

"Of course, it's a BMW," I say aloud, half hoping that he can hear me.

"You're out of order, you, kid!" he barks, pointing a fat, self-important finger in my face, but then, just like the miracle of turning water into wine, the light turns to green.

I smile a big, cheeky grin and turn back to face the man, who's now leaning into my window. "Better get a move on, mate!" I tell him happily.

I take the handbrake off, wink at the balding businessman, who I assume is rather respected and feared in his place of work, and race Black Beauty off the starting line and into the distance.

I can't help but laugh at him again, as he fumbles back into his car, with a long line of angry, late for work commuters behind him, beeping and swearing at him from out of their car windows. If only his colleagues could see him now!

I park my car in a small car park, just around the corner from the college buildings. I look to my right as I get ready to leave and see that I'm parked next to a car belonging to a girl I'm friends with, who is in my first lesson of the day, Drama. She rolls down her window and beckons for me to quickly get into her passenger side seat. I oblige.

"Alright, Holly?"

"Look what I've got!" she insists.

She takes out a pre-rolled spliff from a small compartment under her steering wheel.

"I bought it from this guy in town last night," she explains to me, excitedly.

"Do you know what's in them?" I ask.

"Well, weed obviously, Flic."

She seems quite annoyed that I questioned her about this, so I decide to leave it and let her do what she wants.

"I'm going to smoke it with Emma on Monday, before Drama. It's going to be so funny!" She's already laughing at the idea.

She puts it back in the compartment beneath her steering wheel and we walk to our lesson together.

The lesson is rather uneventful, just talking over exam preparation, and our teacher sets us some homework to create a dramatic monologue for Monday's lesson. I watch the clock as she speaks to the class, wishing time away as I know that, after this, me, Jenk and Len are going to the field to smoke some weed we have left over from the other night. Javan misses out, as he is nowhere to be seen in college today.

I meet Jenk and Len at the front entrance and we walk down the long road exiting the college to the main gates. We sit down in a field behind the car park and start to skin up whilst listening to TT and talking about how excited we are about going to see them in Amsterdam.

We smoke the spliff on a two-puff pass basis, since we're strapped for time.

"Would either of you fancy doing anything more... extreme?" Jenk puts forward the idea, contracting a little bit, considering how we might react.

"What, like skydiving? Not really," I say, frowning and shaking my head as I pass the spliff to Len, who chuckles at my joke.

"No, I mean drugs," Jenk titters.

"Why, what've you got?" Len asks, suddenly very interested.

"Shrooms! Just to get us into the mood for Amsterdam," he proclaims.

We all smile and raise our eyebrows at each other.

Jenk says he'll sort something out for a few days' time, as we don't want to peak too early.

We start walking back to college, the heat from the sun and the lack of air making our high even higher. Before we know it, we're completely stoned. We walk onto the long stretch of straight road into the college again. Through my fits of laughter, I notice that the college building isn't getting any closer. I look down at my feet, just to check that I am actually walking. They definitely look like I'm walking. I look up at the college again and I feel sick as my mind imagines the college zooming out away from me, as if my eyes are camera lenses, attempting to make my life more cinematic.

No thanks.

I stop walking and put my hands on my knees, feeling ill and groaning in confusion and giddiness, with little giggles in between. I look up to find my friends. They're both sitting on the kerb in an even worse state than me. Which, of course, throws me into yet another fit of laughter.

We split off from Len as we get into the building and me and Jenk walk into our media classroom and sit down in our seats. Our mate Ciggsy strolls in with his laptop and sits in the seat in between me and Jenk. He's very small, very fat and very ginger, but he's one of the nicest people you'll meet, despite having the darkest sense of humour ever.

"Alright," he smiles, "where's Ollie?"

Ollie is one of those people in school who you are sure is a serial killer. They walk around the buildings scoping everything out and they always have their heavy, bulky backpack by their side (you've got to be fit to carry an array of weapons around like that all day). He's very quiet and unnerving to speak to. He has short ginger hair, constantly scowling blue eyes that bore into the side of your head whilst you're not looking, and a long green trench coat in which to hide all his additional weapons.

"Just disposing of his last victim, he'll be here soon," I answer.

Our teacher, Gilbert, walks in and briefs us on the overview of the lesson. All we need to do is fill in a sheet with information about films we've watched. Just as she's finishing up, Ollie walks into the room and everybody falls silent.

"Why are you late?" Gilbert asks him, sternly at first.

"I just am," he says, in a very passive aggressive tone, slowly twisting his neck around and staring at her menacingly.

"Okay," she quivers as he goes to sit down.

We start filling out the sheet, me, Jenk and Ciggsy working together to finish it.

We get on to a Mexican film about two lads taking a woman on a trip to a non-existent beach, whilst both battling to get the shag. In the end, they wind up having a threesome and they never speak to each other again.

"You defo got a boner watching that!" Jenk says to Ciggsy.

"No, I didn't." He shakes his head, laughing as he does so.

"You did, to be fair," I join in.

"No I did-*unt!*" he repeats, with extra emphasis.

We just laugh, knowing that he actually did.

After a while, we get bored with filling out the sheet and Ollie has left to go to the toilet, so naturally we start joking about him.

"Bet he just eats pure coleslaw for every meal. That's serial killer food," Ciggsy reckons.

"You know when I had to go to his house to record our short film?" I begin. "Well, he wouldn't let us inside the house, not even into the hall. Probably because the house is littered with dead bodies and coleslaw."

"I can see it now. You turn up at his house and he says, 'We're going to be recording in the basement' and he opens the creaky door to reveal a dark staircase leading down. He makes you lot go first and once you're all inside, he locks the door. And when you turn the lights on there's coleslaw all over the walls," Ciggsy imagines.

"Have you seen that snap bag of coleslaw he carries round for his lunch?" Jenk asks.

"Yeah, he doesn't even use a fork, he just eats it with his bare hands," I follow on.

But we have to stop as Ollie then returns to the table.

Even when he's sat there, Ciggsy tests his luck by telling coleslaw-related stories in front of him; not like he'd know it was about him, unless Cig slipped up and used his name in one of the jokes: "... big fistful of coleslaw and Ollie eats it out of my hand." He stops, stunned by the grave error he just made.

Ollie looks up and his hands slide under the table.

"Is he reaching for his gun or his coleslaw?" I whisper.

The tension is interrupted by Gilbert addressing the class.

"Right, for the second half of the lesson we're going to watch your short films and fill in a feedback form for them all. We'll watch Group One first," she shouts.

Ciggsy turns to me with a worried but amused look on his face. "Oh no!" He laughs.

He is in Group One and I ask him what's wrong, but I can't hear what he whispers in response, and just as I go to ask him to repeat what he said, the short film starts and Gilbert shushes us all.

A minute or so into Ciggsy's film, I remember that a few months ago he asked me to record some audio for the film. He asked me to shout a boy's name and say that dinner was ready. Suddenly, I remember the name that I chose. Ollie.

I tap Ciggsy on the arm and whisper to him, "Now I know what you were worried about. He's defo going to kill us this time."

By now, Jenk has also realised that my cameo appearance is coming up soon.

"Ollie, dinner's ready!" A voice, that is clearly mine, rings through the classroom.

I put my hand over my mouth slowly and I look

at Ciggsy and Jenk who are reacting the same way, before scanning the room. Everybody is looking in our direction with worried expressions, even Gilbert. Everybody is stunned to silence as they wait to see Ollie's reaction. His head slowly turns towards me. His creeping, crabby blue eyes stare deep into my soul as I just stare back, fuelled with the adrenaline of a near death experience.

Thankfully, he just turns back to watch the rest of the film, and everybody else in the class seems to relax and turn back to the screen, too. I'm very lucky to be alive, for now.

I get home and the weed has long since worn off. I sit in the living room with my family and we all ask how each other's days have been as we partially watch a quiz show on TV.

I tell them about my ordeal with the BMW and Laurie finds it hilarious.

"I can't believe you did that!" she quips.

Her shock makes both me and Mum laugh.

Our dad, who was too busy answering questions on the telly, asks us again what we're all laughing at. Mum tells him the story this time while me and Laurie sit together laughing as we review the situation over again.

"Oh Gyod, Flic," he spits in disgust that his darling daughter could do such a thing.

I start to make fun of him for taking it so seriously. "Oh Gyod, Flic!" I echo, pulling my best disgusted face, looking him up and down in disappointment.

We start to laugh again and even Dad emits a reluctant chuckle as he calls me cheeky.

At around eleven o'clock I go upstairs to bed. I watch some TV before I go to sleep.

At 3:00 am, my eyes spring open into a wide stare. I look at my ceiling as I realise that I can't move my arms or legs. I start to panic. The only thing I can do is tilt my head to the side, to look at my slightly open door.

For a moment, nothing happens. Then, slowly, a black, shadow-like hand slides out onto the wall from behind the door.

What follows is a long, thin entity. All black, with two white dots for eyes and a wide white smile.

And all I can do is watch as it slips off the wall and slithers across the floor, out of sight.

I turn my head back to look at the ceiling in an attempt to get away from the horrifying vision. But as I look up, it's there.

Its head is backwards to its body, still displaying the same psychotic smile. Its long, black fingers are stretched out, clinging to the ceiling. It crawls over to the wall above the head of my bed. Creeping so close that our faces are almost touching. I'm desperately trying to move, scream, but I can't do anything.

After what feels like forever, my body rolls over and flies off the bed towards the door. I stand next to the light switch and take one more look at the shadowy being. It's so plain to see. It's on its hands and knees, crouched vertically above my bed and its face snaps in lightning-quick speed to look at me with its menacing smile for one last time, mocking me. I switch on the light and it disappears.

I control my heartbeat and my breathing before turning off the light and getting back into bed.

Looks like my sleep paralysis is back again.

SEVEN DAYS BEFORE:
WOULD YOU BELIEVE?

Monday morning. My alarm blares out its sickening tune at seven o'clock this time.

My weekend consisted of what it always does, going out with Laurie in the afternoon and smoking some weed together, going to work until midnight and then going out with the lads afterwards and smoking some more.

Lying here thinking about these good times prompts me to text Jenk.

Alright, mate, fancy bringing some weed in this morning? Might make our Monday a bit more bearable!

He agrees and says he'll meet me in the car park again.

EPQ is my only real lesson of the day, and we've started watching our presentations in class to coincide with exam month. I present mine on Friday and I'm feeling good about it.

I get showered and dressed and say good morning to all family members present, before reversing out of the drive again and taking the same route to college. No angry BMW driver today.

I get to the car park and Jenk is already there waiting for me. I see Holly's car and remember that she'll be doing the same thing as us today as well. We sit down in the field behind the car park again and Jenk takes out a spliff he's already rolled. He's used some leftovers from Sunday as well, so the spliff is even bigger than usual.

"That's a fat DOINK!" I shout.

We both laugh, remembering the time when an old school friend joined us at the bench and introduced us to the new vocabulary.

We smoke it between the two of us, making us only five minutes late to our lessons.

I say 'bye' to Jenk and walk into the building where my lesson is. The air conditioning is broken in the building and the whole corridor is sweltering hot. I start to feel light-headed, as the heat and the thought of sitting through a load of boring presentations starts to get to me. In turn, I start to feel more and more high and ill the closer I get to the door.

I can't take it anymore and go to turn around; I'll

recover in the café. But I've taken only half a step when my EPQ teacher, Euan, spots me.

"Felicity! We're in this room. As usual."

Like any other Scottish person, everything he says sounds like he hates his life –which he probably does, being an EPQ teacher.

I blow out a hefty amount of air through my lips, just to let him know how much I don't want to be there. I take my usual seat at the back of the class and log onto the computer in front of me. One elbow on the desk, I rest my head on my palm as I watch the first student setting up to present. It's Julian Bucket (pronounced 'Boookaaay', apparently). He was born in Cambridge and his family moved up north to take over a business they inherited, so he sits on his high horse all day, looking down at us northern peasants.

"Go on, Bucket lad!" one of the chavs next to me shouts.

"It's 'Boookaaay'!" he scoffs, in the most camp way possible.

I give a feeble laugh through the pain that I'm feeling. The chav next to me is known around college as 'Scary Lee', due to his extreme height and intimidating appearance. I ask politely if he'll open the window behind his computer, along the side of the classroom. He looks me up and down before saying "Sure" and leaning over to open the window.

"Cheers." I nod at him and he smiles back. Not so scary Lee after all.

41

By this time, the Bucket's all ready to go.

"Hello, class. I'm Julian Boookaaay," he says, with extra emphasis on 'Boookaaay'. He also makes the conscious decision to stare at Scary Lee when he says it. Bad idea. I feel the tables rumble under the force of Scary Lee's blood boiling, but he says nothing. Yet.

"My project is about how influential Shakespeare has been on modern day language," he continues.

Thrilling stuff.

There's no air coming through the windows and I start to become very aware of things happening around me. I hear Scary Lee talking to his mates about how they're going to 'batter' Bucket. I smell the disgusting aroma of cocktail sausages that some excessively overweight girl, who always seems to be eating, has brought into class. And, worst of all, I hear the annoying, monotone, dull, boring, unbearable, droning voice of the little goon that is our dearest Julian Bucket, talking about Shakespeare's use of double negatives. My hands start to shake and become cold but sweaty, and I can't seem to keep my eyes open anymore as everything goes black. In the darkness of my eyes I see swirling patterns, dragging me into a world unknown. I can still hear Bucket; he's asking people which Shakespeare play they think the quote is from. Everybody answers "Romeo and Juliet" because nobody actually cares.

"It was actually... Othello! HEH! Would you believe?" he enthusiastically shouts to the class.

I've never heard anything like it. My jaw drops and my eyes spring back open as all the colour drains from my skin. I don't know whether to laugh or cry.

Euan stops marking Bucket's performance to come over and ask if I'm feeling okay.

"You don't look well, Felicity. You've gone pale." He sounds concerned, even though I can tell he doesn't care whether I'm healthy or not.

"I just need a holiday," I quip. I don't even try to hide the fact that I don't like him, or the fact that I've only just come back from a holiday.

He nods and carries on marking.

I can't get out the door quick enough once the lesson is over. I run straight to the bathroom where I start throwing up. Starting the week off in a positive way. The sweet release makes me feel much better, though. I go to meet Jenk, Jav and Len in the café and spot them occupying a set of sofas in the corner of the room. I flop down in the available space next to Len and rest my head on his knee. He places his hand gently on my head and strokes my hair once and then rests his hand on my shoulder, making me feel immediately better.

"That was the weirdest lesson ever," I mumble, with half of my mouth restricted by Len's knee. They ask why and I reenact it in the best way I can, and they all laugh and agree that Bucket is an absolute weirdo.

I rest my eyes for a few minutes before I have to

go to my drama revision lesson, which makes me feel much better, and the colour finally returns to my face again.

We were asked to prepare a monologue over the weekend for today's lesson. I, of course, have not prepared anything as I've been too busy having terminal cancer to concentrate on putting my heart and soul into my work, only to be graded a C because the teacher hates me. I also couldn't be arsed to do it.

I get to the classroom early, in order to try and come up with an idea last minute. Everyone is already here practising, apart from Holly, but I assume she won't be coming to this lesson. Our teacher, Victoria, struts confidently into the room.

"I hope you've all practiced your monologues over the weekend or you're going to be thoroughly embarrassed when I make you perform to the class," she says, as a snide remark to me, the girl who never writes a monologue but manages to pull it off anyway.

The first person starts their monologue, a nice, cheery piece about a family death. Just as the performance ends and the audience begin to clap, Holly walks in, very visibly high. Her eyes are red, her skin is as white as snow and she's sweating uncontrollably. I wonder to myself why she even bothered to come in.

Vicky recognizes the signs and makes Holly perform her monologue now, as a punishment. She stands in the middle of the room with a big group of students sitting in front of her, looking hopeful and laughing at how awful her performance is going to be.

I sit there watching her cautiously; something isn't right.

She stands there for what seems like forever, sweating and rubbing her hands together. I know what she's going through as I've been there myself: her ears start ringing, her vision begins to blur, and her heart is beating so hard it feels like it's going to burst out of her chest and onto the floor.

Holly's eyes roll backwards, and she collapses, falling onto her back. We hear her head collide with the solid grey floor, sparking an impulse of flinching.

Vicky calls an ambulance as I sit with her, her head in my lap, trying to keep her awake.

We find out that the guy she bought her spliffs from is notorious for spiking his gear with a cocktail of lethal chemicals. He adds date rape drugs like rohypnol and anything else that he can use to cause suffering.

Holly was taken to hospital and had her stomach pumped. Thankfully, she made a quick recovery.

And I didn't have to do a monologue, get in!

(This is where Dad would say "Oh Gyod, Flic!")

· · ·

I walk out of college with Jenk and Len. Jav is already in the car park waiting for us. Len asks me if I'll drive him home today. We go back and forth for a while about why he doesn't just get in with Jav and Jenk, but in the end I decide that it's easier to just drive him rather than argue with him. We get to the car park and Jav gets out of his car once he sees us, and we stand under the full heat of the sun as we talk about getting some shrooms for a week's time.

"I'll ask around if anybody knows where we can buy them from," Jenk says, and I follow up with saying that I'll ask, too.

Javan says he'll bring his camping tent so that we don't have to go home and face our parents when we're tripping out, which we all agree is a good idea.

We get back into our cars and me and Jav chauffeur our friends back home.

I pull up outside Len's house and we both sit there in silence, looking at his house, as if we've never seen it before. He turns to me and I flash him a little smile.

"See you tomorrow then!" I chirp.

He leans over and kisses me on the cheek. He pulls away from me, smiles and says,

"Yeah, see you tomorrow."

I watch him get out of the car and walk to the front door, where he turns around to take one last look at me before he goes inside. There are numerous questions flying around in my head, mostly, "What?!"

I turn the volume back up on my car speakers and of course Tenacious Toes are playing. I set off and hope that I don't crash my car on the way.

Once I get home, I can't wait to tell Laurie about what a strange day I've had. Her car is already on the drive when I arrive, so I go straight up to her bedroom.

"Want to go for a drink?" I ask her.

"Yep," she quips, without a second's hesitation, as she quickly leaps out of the bed and picks up her keys from the bedside table.

We say cheerio to our beloved parents, and head off to the local pub. We get our pint and a half of lager and start racking up the balls on the pool table. I tell her everything, about Bucket, Holly, our quest to find shrooms and my exciting encounter with Len.

"Maybe he likes you?" Laurie shrugs, as it's her turn to break. She pots a blue stripe.

"No way," I say with conviction. I've never been surer about an answer than this one.

"How do you know?" she asks, as she lines up her shot, closing one eye and bending down to level herself with the white ball.

"Come on, Laurie, he's way out of my league, he's beautiful!" I protest.

She laughs at this. She doesn't believe in such things as 'leagues.' She pots another stripe.

47

"It's alright, Laurie, I didn't want to play anyway," I joke, as another stripe is sunk into the pocket adjacent to her.

I finally get my go, potting a fair few spots, but I still lose...

We walk back to the car and skin up in the car park. We smoke in a small, wooded area with a couple of benches dotted around. We sit on a bench, similar to the one we sit on in Paradox Park, and pass the spliff between us. Not long after we start to come up, we see two little white rabbits hopping around on the grass about a meter away. We ogle over how cute they are.

They start to bound away, down a path leading further into the trees.

"How gutted would you be if those were rabbits that could take you to Wonderland and you didn't even follow them," I announce out loud, but not particularly to Laurie, so I don't catch her response. But anyway, I'm too busy imagining what hole these rabbits would take me down to notice anything happening around me.

Tonight is my first night back at work since being diagnosed, so I only have to work for a couple of hours until midnight. I tell my boss, so that he's more understanding about me having so much time off, but

I decide against informing any staff or regulars, for obvious reasons. I throw my jacket under the bar and take a deep breath, looking around at all the familiar faces and seeing how happy they all are.

"Felicity!" I hear somebody shout in a booming Scottish accent.

I look around and see exactly who I was expecting to see, my least favourite customer, Francis, scowling and shaking his empty pint glass at me.

I just nod at him and walk around to the bigger side of the bar, where the cider pump is, and pour his pint. I bring it back around to him and place it carefully in front of him.

"Is that everything?" I ask with a reluctant smile.

"That's not going to do now, is it?" he says in his condescending manner, staring exaggeratedly at the drink.

So, I go back to the other side and pour him another pint.

"How's that?" I force a polite smile again as I speak to him.

To which he just shakes his head and tells me to put it onto his tab.

I click on his name on the touchscreen till, and add two pints of cider to his tab, muttering "dickhead" under my breath as I do it.

The pub is busier than usual during the dinner rush and I'm constantly running back and forth, between customers, without a single break, for almost two hours. I keep getting bouts of dizziness and several times I feel as though I might pass out. I feel my phone vibrate in my pocket, so I pull it out slightly, just to check what the notification is. It's a text from Mum asking me how I'm feeling at work.

"I think I'm more important than your phone. Go and get me a pint," Francis orders, in the nicest way he knows how.

I stare at him, remaining motionless for a moment until I feel as if he is uncomfortable enough for me to move on. I ask my colleague, Karen, to do it instead, which she does, and I decide to stay on the opposite bar for a while, so I don't have to look at him again.

It doesn't take long before my boss comes over to me.

"Flic, Francis says you've ignored him," he queries with his head on the side.

A small, softly-spoken, older man with grey hair and blue eyes, he's very understanding, a great boss, but he will never, under any circumstances, go against what a regular says.

I raise my eyebrow and let out a hefty laugh.

"Daniel, I wouldn't ignore someone, especially not a customer. I just asked Karen to do his pint for me because he wasn't happy with the way I was doing it, apparently," I explain.

"Well, alright, just serve him yourself next time, and don't ignore the customers," he reiterates - I mustn't have been speaking English.

. . .

The rest of the night unfolds uneventfully, apart from Francis using his 'buzz sentence' again; "I think I'm more important than (blank). Go and get me a pint."

But he soon leaves, thankfully, and the pub suddenly becomes very hollow and eerie with no customers at all on the smaller side of the bar. Not for long, though, as a group of four middle-aged regulars walk through the front door, shouting and laughing together.

"Hi, Flic! Three pints of 'diet beer' and a large white please!" one of them shouts, over the noise they're creating themselves.

After they pay for the drinks, they sit down on the table closest to the bar. The only woman in the group, who just happens to be Len's auntie, turns around in her chair to face me.

"Hiya, love, you okay? Are you still knocking around with our Len?" she asks, with a smirk and a wink.

"Yeah, I am," I laugh, knowing what the conversation is going to be about already.

"Have you managed to pin him down yet?"

"Not yet, Lisa, I'm working on it though!" I smile and point at her in a confident way.

"What are you talking about?" asks a male member of the group, Phillip, a man with short white hair, spiked up to create a Great Wall of fringe above his forehead, and piercing, bright blue eyes that stare into your soul and seem to locate your deepest secrets. His face is deeply wrinkled but not in an unattractive way, and he is well aware of it, often using his self-proclaimed 'good looks' to seduce women of all ages. But I see through his charismatic façade of "yeah man, life's short, gotta live it to the max, yano?" and see him for what he really is, a man who enjoys injecting people's lives with pain.

"She fancies my nephew, Len. We're hoping he plucks up the courage to ask her out soon!" she chirps, like we're two schoolgirls gossiping about our dream boy.

"Don't go out with him, go out with me. I'm more experienced." He winks at me.

I see the devilish twinkle in his eyes.

"I'm alright, thanks," I laugh, scrunching up my face.

"Seriously, I'll take you out for dinner," he replies, more seriously this time.

"Seriously, I'm alright," I repeat myself, my voice a bit sterner this time in order to get the message across.

It must have worked because he laughs it off and the conversation moves on.

Not long afterwards, the new waitress, a young girl called Mae, fourteen years old to be exact, walks past their table with a couple of plates in each hand to serve to a couple in another room. Phillip stares at her arse casually as she passes. She walks back through empty-handed and Phillip starts up a conversation with her.

"Well, hello... Who might you be?" he questions the girl, with his head tilted forward slightly so that he's looking up at her from beneath his brow bone.

"I'm Mae, I started last week," she replies innocently.

"Are you good at your job?" he asks, in his soft but slightly creepy voice.

"Ha-ha, yeah, I think so. I'm trying my best, anyway!" she grins.

"Oh! I bet you are. Bet you've got a few secrets in that pinny of yours." He smirks and nods in reference to the small black pinafore she has tied around her waist.

But the group, and the girl, just laugh it off and she walks back into the kitchen.

Why did nobody else find that weird and inappropriate? I decide to keep my thoughts to myself since nobody else picked up on it, but I go into the kitchen and talk to Mae about the types of people that come in here, and that I'll help her out if she needs me to. When I get back to the bar, Phillip is propped up against it, waiting for me. He starts asking me questions while I'm obliged to spend an eternity pouring four pints for him; there's no getting away now.

"So. Whereabouts do you live?" he asks.

"Around."

"Here?"

"Not far from here."

"Culcherry?" he guesses.

"Nah."

"Where then?" he demands that I tell him.

"Twenty-four, ninety-five, please." I ask for the payment as I set the last pint down.

He reluctantly hands over the payment in five-pound notes and change before going to sit back down.

Midnight finally arrives, and my shift is over. I shout goodnight to my boss and walk out from behind the bar.

"'Night, guys," I say to Lisa and the rest of the group, sparking multiple "goodnight's" in return, including from Phillip.

"Goodnight, Flic, come give us a kiss." He closes his eyes and pouts at me.

I stare for a moment, not knowing what to say or do.

"Wouldn't want to upset Len," I chuckle and start to walk away.

"Are you out in the village tonight?" he asks, as he does every night that I see him.

"Sure am," I answer, continuing to exit both the bar and the conversation.

Phillip's glassy eyes follow me all the way to the front door. I make eye contact with him as I turn around and slowly shut the door. He continues to stalk me with his gaze even when I'm outside. He's completely spun around in his chair just to watch me walk past the crown glass windows.

It may be a slight overreaction, but I decide to lock my car doors and not dawdle in the car park for too long. I hope I don't have nightmares about him tonight.

3 DAYS BEFORE:

THE INFINITY POOL

F riday is usually a good day for me since I don't have to be in college for long. All I have to do today is present my EPQ presentation. But not this Friday. Instead of the usual ripple of my alarm, I'm woken by excruciating pain, leading me to throw up before I have the chance to do anything other than race to the bathroom and stick my head down the loo. I open my eyes as my mum comes in and rubs my back. The toilet is covered in blood, with remnants of it still pouring out of my mouth and dripping off my chin. I look at Mum and she looks very concerned, as you'd expect. However, the doctors said this is a common symptom, so she tells me that she'll ring into college for me and she puts me back into bed with a bottle of water.

It's not long before everybody has left for work

and I'm left alone. I take my antibiotics and fall back to sleep.

I wake up at 1 p.m. feeling a whole lot better, so naturally, I roll myself a spliff and lie down on the wicker chairs outside. I close my eyes and feel the stinging heat of the midday summer sun on my eyelids and all over my clammy, pale skin and take a drag of the spliff. Relax.

As I lie there, alone, I start to think about my friends. It wouldn't be fair if I just died without telling them. I'm also starting to feel secluded in my illness and I need to tell those closest to me. I concoct a plan to tell each one individually, starting with the only member of the group who is most likely not in college either, Javan. So, I swiftly text him as I'm walking back into the house to get a shower.

Hiya Jav, are you off college today?

After around five seconds of pressing send, I receive a reply: *Yeh.*

Are you alright? I respond to his blunt text, despite him giving off the vibe that he doesn't feel like talking right now.

Just having a bad day.

I'll come round and see you, yeah? I've got something to tell you. I'll bring round a little present for you.'

Okay.

Great chatting with you, Jav.

I get a quick shower and dry off before walking

back into my bedroom to get dressed. As I swing open one of my black mirrored wardrobe doors, I see two little white feet stood next to me in the image created in the adjoining door. I turn my head to see, but nothing is there. I continue to stare in the roundabout spot where the feet were, with my red, glassy eyes and for some reason they keep falling to the same position, a few inches below where my eyeline is, as if I'm subconsciously holding eye contact with somebody. I move closer to the spot and I can feel the blunt presence of a person standing there. I hold my hand out in front of me and the air feels deathly cold. I take a step back into my original position.

"Hiya, mate... Don't mind me... Just getting a T-shirt out of here, no wukkas, ha-ha..." I announce, pretending not to be scared and taking a T-shirt out of the wardrobe.

I close the door and start to shuffle out, not turning my back on 'the spot'.

"I'm going out now, so make yourself at home... What's mine is yours... TV remote's on the side there if you want to watch some telly or something." I point to 'the spot' where it can find the remote, as I edge further and further out of the door.

"Alright, see you later, mate... Have fun... 'Bye."

I shut the door behind me.

I need to stop doing drugs.

• • •

I walk to Jav's as it's only around the corner and I let myself in, knowing he will be wrapped up in bed, which he is. When I enter his bedroom, I say nothing. I stare at him and the depressed look on his face and I hold up the spliff.

"Here's one I rolled earlier!" I shout enthusiastically like a children's TV presenter.

Thankfully, it makes him crack a little smile and I tell him to get dressed and we'll go to Paradox Park to smoke it. Within five minutes we're out the door and on a scenic walk through the park.

"So, how are you feeling, Jav? Why such a bad day? It's only two o'clock. What can go so wrong?" I ask him, concerned.

"Nothing's happened... It's just how I feel," he mumbles quietly.

I spark up the spliff and have a few puffs before passing it over.

"This'll sort you out." I try to encourage him to feel better.

We sit down together on a little wooden bench and he tells me more about himself than he ever has done in the twelve years I've known him.

"It's like I've lost myself. I don't know who I am anymore, and I don't know who I'm going to be. It's scary, Flic," he confesses.

"Nobody knows who they're going to be, Jav. That's the fun of it."

"But it's not fun. There are so many things that

can go wrong at any point in the future. What if I become homeless? Or, at the age of forty, I might die a long, slow, painful death and lose everything I've worked on for my entire life?" he questions, not expecting me to have an answer to his certain epiphany.

"Well... All I can say is that you should worry about the future when you get there. Live your life now instead of worrying about things yet to come. I want us all to have a really great year together, Javan. Please," I plead.

He says nothing, just looks up at me momentarily before dropping his head back down in between his hands, which are propped up by his bony elbows, leaning on his even bonier knees.

"Look Javan, I got some bad news when I came back off holiday and I really need to tell you guys but I want to do it when the time is right for everybody, so I need you to promise me that you won't tell Jenk or Len," I order, in the nicest way possible.

"I promise I won't. What's happened?" he replies, intrigued, rising from his hunched over position to turn slightly and face me.

"Well, do you remember I told you about how I couldn't stop throwing up ever since my holiday?" I start.

"Yeah..." he anticipates.

"I went to see a doctor about it, and I had to have loads of tests and... well... he told me that I'm

60

probably going to die before the end of the year, mate," I explain to him.

His eyes dart around for a moment before his head slowly creeps back into the miserable solace of his hands. We say nothing for a while, just sit there listening to the sweet sound of birds tweeting in the treetops and the cars driving past on the road behind the trees.

"I can't believe it, Flic... What's going to happen?" he asks, uncertain as to whether he wants to know the answer or not.

"I really don't know, Jav... But what I do know is that this is going to be the best summer of my life, and I want you three to be there with me for it." I smile reassuringly at him and put a hand on his leg.

"Okay, Flic," he says, as he attempts a frail smile, trying to hold back his tears.

As we start to walk back to the car park, we get to a long, narrow pathway, guarded either side by thick foliage. A few meters ahead of us, I spot a tall man standing next to the side of the path. He has a black hood covering his face and a small black dog running around his feet. I turn to look at Jav, who is looking down at his feet as he kicks them out in front of him. I look back up at the man, but he isn't there. I look around at the side of the pathway and there's nowhere he could have gone unless he's just decided to walk via the mangroves. Jav and I finally get to the spot where the man stood, and I look to my left. He's standing in a flat patch of grass on the other side of the trees, I can barely see him through it, but I can make out that he's standing still and facing our way. I keep my eyes on him as we continue to walk along the path.

Suddenly, just as we become level with him, he turns and starts to walk in the same direction as us (despite it being the direction he came from originally).

"Shall we go down there?" I signal to Jav, meaning the tiny path that leads onto a close of houses.

He shrugs and agrees, and I quickly divert to the right, away from the man. I decide not to tell Jav, just so that I don't panic him.

We get into the close and I sigh with a sense of relief, though I'm sure it was nothing to worry about. As we get to the end of the road, I hear the tinkle of a dog collar behind us. My head snaps around to look and so does Jav's. it's the same man. He's followed us again... I stop in my tracks and lean closer to get a better look at his face.

Is that Phillip?

As soon as he realises I've spotted him, he runs into an adjacent pathway, his little dog tootling along behind him.

8:00 p.m. My phone lights up with a message from Jenkies in the group chat:

Found this new sick place to smoke. I've already got the drugs so let's just meet in half an hour and I'll direct us. And remember... Finesse, never stress!

Sounds good to me!

I set off in the Black Beauty and pick Len up from his house as Jav drives to Jenk's and we all meet up together, me and Len in one car, Jav and Jenk in the other, at the front.

We drive at high speed for around fifteen minutes down unlit, winding country roads, until I see Jav's little blue car slow down and pull over into what is pretty much a ditch, halfway along an empty country road, surrounded by trees and farmer's fields.

"Surely not?" Len scoffs.

Jenk and Jav appear from the car, carrying camping chairs over each shoulder.

"Let's go, gang!" Jenkies shouts in a preppy American accent, as he trudges along the road and past my car.

We follow behind him as he leads us up to a metal gate, which I'm guessing was put there for the purpose of not letting people in. But regardless, we scale it with ease and continue down the dirt path.

"Where the hell are you taking us, Jenkies?" Len enquires in a joking manner.

"You'll see," Jenk replies, turning around and nodding with a smirk.

He puts a spliff into his mouth and lights it, taking a few puffs before passing it to Jav.

Already stoned, we walk along the path, which is narrowly enclosed on either side by tall hedges, with nothing to see but what appears to be an endless dirt track ahead of us, and the sultry night sky hanging above us. Dusk is fast giving way to night and, as the sun recedes, a full moon appears to illuminate our way.

I begin to think about telling Jenkies and Len about my terminal dilemma. I open my mouth, ready to start with the words, "I have something to tell you...." but I'm rudely interrupted by the hissing of a large black cat emerging from the hedge. Its back is arched, its hackles up and it has a menacing look in its big blue eyes as it presents its long, sharp, dagger-like fangs to us. We all scream and begin to run away, lifting our feet as high up off the ground as we can, away from the ferocious feline, as it follows closely behind.

Once I feel like I've made good distance between me and the cat, I calm down and look behind me. The cat hasn't been there for God knows how long. I turn around to look at the rest of them and they're still jumping around and screaming in terror.

"It's gone!" I shout through laughter

They, too, calm down and stand still, looking

around their feet to check that I'm not lying before shrugging it off and laughing, and we continue to walk to our destination.

Eventually, we come to a hill and Jenk stops and admires it.

"Is this it?" Jav asks, unimpressed.

"Up," Jenk says with a smile, before pushing himself up the hill and over the top.

The rest of us obligingly follow him. On the other side of the hill, there's a narrow wooden plank, clinging to the banks either side of a small river.

"That's at least an eighty-foot drop! You don't expect me to walk over that, do you, Jenkies?" Len shouts dramatically.

"Len, it's probably about a six-foot drop, and yes, you're going over it," Jenk orders.

Jenkies goes over first, his long arms outstretched either side of him for balance. Thankfully, the plank doesn't snap. Jav goes next, making it across safely. Then it's my turn. I'm already nervous because of my terrible balance on flat surfaces, but I step up to the plank, Jav and Jenk eagerly waiting on the other side. I float across, making it look easy, feeling proud of myself for not falling in. Lastly, Len is pacing back and forth on the other side of the bank, panicking.

"Come on, Len, it's safe!" Javan reassures him.

"It's defo gonna snap on me now, though!" he predicts.

After a long discussion, he finally musters up the

courage to walk across. He steps sideways slowly, about one step per minute, in fact, and the plank shows no signs of snapping, or even bending slightly at all.

As Len finally gets to the middle of the plank, Jenkies puts his foot onto the edge of it and starts making the plank wobble in between the banks. We all start laughing as Len starts to panic again.

"JENK – JENKIES – STOP! STOP IT!" he barks as he starts to topple over, balancing himself with windmilling arm motions.

I am laughing so hard that I can't make a sound, doubled over, leaning on a slab of stone sticking out of a hill of mud. Making me laugh even more is the sound of Jenk's hysterical laughter

"HOH-HOH-HOH-HOH!" he guffaws, almost falling to the ground as Len pushes past him, all too eager to step off the plank.

Javan walks up the small hill and finds the picturesque setting Jenkies has dragged us all this way to get to see.

"Aww, this is nice, Jenkies!" he coos, and we all come to join him.

We sit down on a small ledge of dried mud and take in the view. A circle of trees stand sentry around a lake, their silhouettes reflected in the mirror-like surface of the water, together with the exceptionally bright full moon and a scattering of twinkling stars. We revel in the beauty of the moonlight dancing across the ripples of the mysterious, dark water, created by anonymous small fish bobbing around in the unknown

"Guys..." Javan starts.

We all peel our stares from the lake and turn to face Jav.

"I've been looking at this lake for a while now... and... it looks like a black hole... Yano, like... the bottom of the earth..." he explains.

We all look back at the lake, eager to see if we can imagine it, too.

Unfortunately, we can.

"Errrrr! Noooo, I don't like it! I feel so close to the edge now! I'm going to fall off!" I panic, laughing and simultaneously feeling like I could cry, and I start to shuffle my feet backwards, despite being a good meter away from the edge of the lake.

Everybody else starts doing the same, laughing and screaming. Jav walks over to the edge and dangles his foot over the spine-chilling black hole.

"I'm going to fall through space for eternity!" he announces.

"Jav, don't!" Len pleads, with a hint of actual worry evident in his voice.

Jav laughs and sits back down as Jenk lights another spliff.

We sit silently for a moment, listening to the relaxing sounds of the lake and all the creatures that live in and around it.

I look up at the full moon that has a slight line of shading across the top right curve and I follow Jav's train of thought.

"Guys..." I duplicate Jav's opening statement of a few moments before. They all turn to look at me, just as we had done previously in response to Jav. "If you look at the moon like that... it looks like a small opening with the lid slightly ajar... yano, like... as if we lived inside a globe..."

"Flic!" Len shouts as they all look up at the moon and understand what I'm talking about and we all start to scream and laugh again.

After a few hours (and a few spliffs), we start to head back. It's quite dark and I'm constantly on edge, thinking I'm going to fall and die from the many obstacles we have ahead of us. Walking across a thin plank, climbing a hill and scaling a gate are all a lot harder to do when you're seeing double and can hardly keep your balance. But thankfully, we all manage to make it back to the cars without serious injury. We all give Jav a fist bump and say goodbye as he gets into his car alone and drives off. I follow him, with Len in the passenger seat and Jenkies in the back. Javan isn't making it easy for me to keep up, though. He speeds ahead of me along the dark country lanes. Needing to stay behind him, I speed up, too, making the car slightly harder for me to control. I slowly start to drift over to the other side of the road, my wheels shuddering over the illuminated cat's eyes in the middle of the two lanes. Jenk and Len start to ridicule me,

"OOOOOOOOOOOOOOH!" they chorus, building up the volume of their voices.

"Stop it! You're making it worse!" I shout, whilst trying hard to concentrate.

But they continue to get louder and louder. Jenkies even sits forwards and hangs onto the back of Len's chair in order to get closer to my ear.

"I'm not joking! We're going to crash if you keep doing it," I explain, as the wheels continue to collide with the cat's eyes.

All I can see through the windscreen is darkness and rows of trees rushing past, as my car whips around bends and flies down straight stretches of road. But their jeering soon stops as the headlights of an oncoming car flood the road ahead of us.

"Flic, move over now," Jenk orders.

"I'm trying!" I reply, panicked.

The deafening rhythmic thud of the cat's eyes under my wheels seems to become louder and more nagging, the closer we get to the car in front. Soon, their headlights blind us all as we approach one another. At the last second, I manage to swerve back onto my side of the road and the thudding stops as we're back on the right side of the road.

Inside the car echoes with silence as Jenk and Len sit back in their seats, stunned, their eyes wide with fear.

"We just nearly died," I say, lucky to be there to voice what, moments before, had seemed inevitable.

That was the only sentence spoken for the remainder of the journey.

I pull up onto the kerb outside Jenk's house and we sit there silently for a moment, contemplating our own mortality, before Jenk opens the door and hangs one leg out onto the pavement.

"See ya... love you..." he whispers to us both.

"'Bye, Jenkies, love you..." we both reply.

He shuts the door and we watch him walk inside.

Len asks me to stay over at his house tonight, since we nearly died. I accept, as there's no better excuse than a near death experience, and so I drive around the corner to his house and we walk inside without saying another word.

THE DAY:
A MIND-BLOWING WHITEY

I t's Monday morning and I have to be in college for nine o'clock to present my EPQ presentation. If a terminal illness can't get you an A*, I don't know what can. It's only me and Jenkies that need to be in college today. He's in a six-hour graphics exam, so I can only imagine how bored he is.

I walk into the classroom and eye up my seat, but there's somebody already in it. He's a small Indian guy with glasses and a chinstrap beard that's confused about which chin it should sit under. I've never seen him before in here, so I decide to cut him some slack and go onto the computer next to my usual one. I sit down and he slowly swivels his head toward me.

"Alright." I nod.

He doesn't reply, just slowly turns back to his

screen. I have a peek at it myself to spot his name: Mehzah.

The presentation before mine is about the different swear words that are associated with which gender, one of the more interesting ones.

"So, there are some swear words that women should never say, according to some," the presenter states.

"Yeah, like gunt," Mehzah says, sending the whole room into fits of laughter.

"Yeah, like that..." the presenter laughs and swiftly moves on.

When the presentation is drawing to a close, Mehzah leans over to me and whispers to me with unblinking eyes. "Wanna see a dead body, bro?"

"*What...?* No." I frown and shake my head at him.

He shrugs and turns back to his computer.

Everybody claps and it's my turn to present.

I set up my presentation on the projector and look around the room at my peers.

"Hello, my name is Felicity and my presentation is based on the different effects of drugs on the mind and the body," I reveal to them, my initial slide being covered in tiny images of weed leaves and bongs.

I hear Bucket and his mate sniggering and nudging each other.

"As you can see, my presentation is already more interesting than most." I glare at Bucket and he cowers behind his friend.

I click to the next slide. It's headed *ECSTASY*.

"In low moderation," I tell the class, "pill poppers may experience feelings of wellbeing, empathy, closeness to others and an increase in confidence and energy. However, like every drug, it has its bad side effects, such as: poor muscle control, paranoia or increased blood pressure. In higher doses, MDMA can lead to an overdose, or, if you're not a little bitch..." I wink and point at Bucket, "... you may experience a floating sensation, hallucinations and irrational or bizarre behaviour instead," I cite, in my best presentation voice.

"The science behind the effects of MD on the brain is that it causes a greater release of serotonin and norepinephrine than of dopamine. Serotonin is a neurotransmitter that plays an important role in the regulation of mood, pain and other behaviours. The excess release of serotonin causes the mood-elevating effects people experience. But experiments show that high doses can damage the nerve cells that contain serotine, meaning that ecstasy may leave long-term damaging effects on the brain," I conclude on the subject of MDMA.

Throughout my presentation, Scary Lee doesn't take his eyes off me. He even applauds at the end of the presentation, which he hasn't done for anybody previously. I sit down in my seat, a few down from his, and he leans over and whispers to me, "That was great, Flic," as he flashes a white grin.

I smile back and say, "Thanks", trying to hide the puzzled look on my face.

As the lesson ends, I walk over to Euan to ask for my grade.

"Well, Felicity. I hope you didn't get all of that information from firsthand account." He raises a suspicious eyebrow.

"Definitely not," I laugh.

"Well, I'm happy to give you an A for your presentation. I haven't marked your written work yet so I can't give you an overall grade, but I'd say you can be expecting an A*." He smiles.

I didn't think Scottish people knew how to smile.

I begin to walk out of the classroom, and I feel my phone vibrate in my pocket. It's a text from Jenkies in the group chat:

We've got the shrooms for tonight! Finesse, never stress!

Straight away, a reply from Len causes my phone to vibrate again:

Get in, Jenkies laaaa.

My phone vibrates for a third time. It's from Jenk, asking me to meet him in the café, which I do.

He is sitting at a little, wooden, square table with two seats either side of it. He has his back to me but his long, dangly legs are visible either side of the chair, and his trusty bucket hat always makes him easily identifiable. I sit down across from him and ask how he's doing. We chat about his exam and my presentation, which brings us onto the subject of tonight.

"Do you reckon we should bring anything else?" He smirks.

"I'll bring some weed as well, just to be safe," I confirm, and he appreciates the gesture.

"Also, Jenkies, there's something I've been meaning to tell you, but I haven't really had the chance before," I begin. He looks concerned but intrigued simultaneously.

"When I got back off holiday, I had to go to the doctor's, and they told me that I have until the end of the year to live..." I explain.

He sits there and stares at me for a while before he says one word and one word only:

"Fuck!"

"Yeah, I know. That's why I really want the rest of this year to be sick! So, we're going all out tonight and every night for the rest of the year, yeah?" I ask, already knowing what his response will be.

"Yeah!" he proclaims.

"I haven't told Len yet, though, so try not to say anything in front of him."

"Why? Do you want it to be a surprise?" He smirks as he tries not to laugh.

"That's the one, Jenkies, that's the one!"

I get home at four o'clock and I'm not feeling my best after my first day back at college in a while, so Laurie insists that we go out for a doink to cheer me up. It doesn't take much for me to cave, and five minutes later, we're walking through the park in search of a bench to sit on.

Once settled, we begin our deep and meaningful stoned conversations. She asks if I've made any progress with Len yet and I lie and say no, I don't want to jinx anything just yet.

"Have you told them about your illness yet?" she asks me wearily.

"I told Jav a few days ago when we were out together, and I told Jenkies at college today, but I haven't really had the opportunity to tell Len yet," I explain.

"Well, you better do it soon before it's too late and he finds out the hard way," she lectures, in her older sister way.

I chuckle and agree, then we fall into a companionable silence. Me thinking about how and when I'm going to tell Len. And Laurie thinking about how much she's going to miss her little sister once she's gone.

"I can't wait for Amsterdam, though!" I proclaim, trying to lighten the mood.

"Aw, I know, I'm jealous!" she replies, plastering a fake smile on her face to mask the sadness in her eyes.

"Do you want to see the list of songs they're going to play?" I ask.

"Yeah, go on then."

I take out my phone and go onto the Tenacious Toes social media page in search of the set list.

Just as I find it, my phone goes blank.

"What the...? It was on fifty percent!" I protest.

"We'll get going now, anyway, yeah?" she says, as she stands up and turns away from me, wiping away the small tear that falls from her eye.

As we're walking back, a group of young lads are walking in our direction. As we get closer, I recognize one of them as being Scary Lee, meaning that the rest of them are his equally scary mates. We continue to walk on, minding our own business, when the group stops in front of us.

"Give us all ya stuff. NOW," a tall, skinny, hooded member of the group demands.

"All I've got is a broken phone," I say, and I take it out of my pocket and show them the blank screen.

Scary Lee finally recognizes me once I speak and he steps forward in front of the rest of the group.

"What's happened to it?" he quizzes.

"I don't know. It just stopped working and this screen won't go away now," I explain.

"Ah. Give it here, I think I know what the problem is." He takes my phone out of my hand and fiddles around with the buttons. He turns the phone around to show me that the screen is fully functional

77

again. The hooded rascal reaches out to take the good-as-new phone out of Scary Lee's hand, but he pushes his hand away and passes it back over to me.

"Oh... Thanks, Lee." I nod in appreciation.

"No problem, Flic. Come on," he motions to the rest of the group, and our hooded foes scowl at us as we cross paths and they follow him, presumably to locate an alternative target.

"What the hell was that all about?" Laurie laughs.

"No idea," I whisper. I turn around and look back at the group and see that Scary Lee is already looking back at me.

I drive to Paradox Park and meet the rest of the group, who are already there. We sit down at our favourite picnic bench and roll a spliff. Jenkies pulls out a giant 'snap bag' containing hundreds of pieces of what looks like a tree's haemorrhoids. Len grabs the bag and examines the shrooms inside, as if he's some sort of drug critic.

"Ready?" Jav begins, to which we all reply, "Yes!"

We all swallow a handful of shrooms each and start to pass the spliff around.

Len is visibly nervous, but, in order to retain street cred, he is also very visibly trying to hide it. Jav looks as though he'd rather be tucked up in a ball in the shower than be here taking shrooms with us. He's sat in a sulk, his elbow perched on the tabletop, his chin desperately balancing atop a skinny, twisted arm. Jenkies is chill, nodding his head slowly to the mellow tune floating out of the tiny speaker, into our wanting ears.

A blinding bright light intrudes on our bench of tranquility and we all look in the direction of the car, squinting.

"Is that a car?" Len asks.

Yes, it is. And the headlights are on full beam in our direction. The car door slams shut and a person approaches us. I watch them walk closer, their features shadowed by the light rising behind them.

"Ryan?" a woman's voice shouts

"No," Len replies.

"Is Ryan here?" the woman asks again, walking right up to the bench and staring at us all.

I join in. "No, he's not. We don't know anyone called Ryan, either."

"Are you sure you don't know where he is?" she reiterates.

"We're sure!" Jav snaps, from behind his hood.

"Well... If you see him, tell him to come home," she quickly finishes up and walks away.

We can hear her husband shouting over to her to ask if she's found him, and she replies that she hasn't. They get back into the car and drive away, probably going to another stoner hotspot to look for him.

Eventually, we come to the conclusion that Ryan must be the boy from the year below us in high school, the one who's always getting himself into trouble and running away from home. I hope they find him soon.

A mere ten minutes later, Len shouts, "Whoa!" with a look of fear in his eyes. I follow his gaze to identify the ghost he has clearly just seen, but instead I'm faced with a hooded figure walking towards the bench. I imagine it's just someone else looking for Ryan.

"It's alright, ya know meh!" the shadow whispers to us. "It's me, Gaz, ya know meh!" he repeats.

I don't know anyone named Gaz, let alone someone who walks around a park like this at night.

He stumbles up to the bench and flings himself onto the seat next to Len so that I can't see him properly anymore. He shushes us and we all fall silent.

"The police are out lookin' for meh," he kindly informs us, in an unsettling, hushed voice.

We all look at each other worriedly, but after a few seconds, Jav asks why.

"Just kicked our kid's head in, he owes meh moneh," he explains, in an eerily calm voice.

We sit in silence, none of us really knowing how to react. Every so often he becomes jumpy and tell us to be quiet, or asks us if we can hear something, which we can't, so it's obvious he's off his head and paranoid as fuck. He asks if he can have any of the spliff we were passing around. Len gives it to him, planning on not smoking any more of it after Gaz has had his dirty trap around the roach.

As he sparks the lighter, I take the opportunity to look at his face. The lighter held below his face creates the same effect as when you would hold a torch under your chin whilst telling a scary story when you were younger, making him look even more terrifying. He looks to be in his late twenties and has bright blue eyes and olive skin, covered in the graves of his previously deep-set acne. His eyes are darting around and bloodshot and are being caressed by heavy dark rings beneath them, as if he hasn't slept in months.

It falls silent again once Gaz has lit the spliff. Every time he lifts his arm, I flinch, thinking he's swinging for Len, who is holding my hand, squeezing it every time Gaz moves, indicating that he's feeling the same anxiety as I am.

"So, h-h-h-how o-o-o-o-o-old a-are y-you, the-e-e-en?" Len stutters in fear.

"Shhhh... twenny-sixxx..." Gaz replies, whispering again, thinking the police are crouched under the bench, ready to jump out on him at any minute.

I've never seen Len so scared before but Jav and Jenkies seem to be fine.

In an attempt to prompt us to leave, Len asks, "Is that the last one?" referring to the spliff that Gaz just threw into the bushes.

"Nah, we've got loads left!" Jenk replies.

Me and Len both look at each other in the darkness, with expressions on our faces that read, 'for fuck's sake, we're dead.'

But thankfully, after what feels like forever, Gaz finally says that he better leave, in case the police turn up. He gets up from the bench and gives us one warning. "If the police come, you didn't see anything, alright?" he instructs, rather than asks.

"Yeah, no problem," we all reply.

And he walks off further into the forest.

"What the fuck?" Jenk whispers.

Javan doesn't seem to be remotely fazed as we contemplate leaving, but in the end, we decide not to, because there's nowhere else for us to go. So, we just try to put it to the back of our minds and enjoy the night.

I close my eyes and tilt my head back, feeling the warm summer breeze caress my face. It's only been about twenty minutes since we took the shrooms but I'm already becoming impatient waiting for the high, trying anything to reduce the anticipation.

"I was watching this programme today, right? How mad is this? Everything in this world... isn't real. Boom. What!" I state, completely out of the blue.

"... What?" Len shakes his head and pulls an overly confused faced.

"Because, right, you know how it's scientifically proven that nobody sees the same shade of a colour as anybody else does, so basically everything we see is just any object that we give shape and colour to, that we name, that we give purpose to."

"Flic, shut up!" Jenkies interrupts.

Everybody turns to look at him, suddenly hunched over with his head down, almost below the table, and his hood up.

"You alright?" Jav mumbles.

Jenkies, as I've said before, is a boy of few words, and so instead of answering, "No, I'm not alright," he throws up without moving at all.

"Whoa! He's gone too far west!" I shout, getting up from the bench and walking a few steps away.

Len does the same, but Jav just sits back away from Jenk. I can feel the lump forming in my throat the more I think about it. I really don't want us all to have a bad trip; I can't think of anything worse, in fact.

I give him a piece of chewie from my pocket and he drinks some water, and thankfully he says he feels loads better.

"Maybe you should have another shroom, Jenkies, la!" Len jokes.

Despite it being a joke, he takes another one.

After another half an hour, the shrooms start to hit me. I close my eyes and start to hallucinate.

All I see is black, until I tilt my head straight and suddenly, a circle of giant cartoon elephants, standing on two legs with flashing, colourful, neon Aztec print bouncing across their entire bodies, start dancing around me. Their trunks are swinging around in front of them, narrowly avoiding hitting me in the face, and so I'm trying to dodge out of the way. I'm scared, but also enjoying the trip at the same time. The elephants fly away above me and they flip over, standing reasonably further away from me now. Horse-drawn carriages, in the same style as the elephants, start to bounce in, flashing neon colours, dancing and moving in time with the elephants. More fairytale objects join the circle and soon, I'm surrounded by hundreds of flashing, dancing cartoons, all around me.

Meanwhile, Len closes his eyes and sees his life playing out through quick, flashing scenes, each one in a different style. He sees his family in the living room, celebrating Christmas, but they're all portrayed by a star-studded cast of puppets. Then he sees himself, me, Jav and Jenk sitting at this bench, but we're all dressed as pirates. And he's the captain! We get up from the bench and run towards the ocean where the biggest ship you've ever seen is docked up in the distance.

"Come on, Captain!" Jenkies shouts, motioning for Len to get into the little rowing boat with the rest of us. When we get to the ship, the crew of pirates is singing a song about him whilst they work on the deck. He stands at the wheel and takes a deep breath, and he can actually taste the salt in his mouth.

Jenkies' trip comes next. He closes his eyes and he's watching a jagged cartoon on a purple animated television; the intro tune fades out and he and Len are having a competition to see who can do the coolest trick, jumping off this twenty-foot cliff. Me and Jav are sat motionless and unblinking on a rock, watching them with emotionless smiles on our faces, as if the animators were strapped for time on the deadline of the short sketch. Len jumps first. He does a couple of forward flips and lands on the yellow sand below. Jenk jumps off the edge of the cliff, doing back flips and front flips, before landing perfectly. Len's face turns menacing and he demands a rematch. They walk back up to the top and Len jumps off again, doing better than last time. Seconds after Jenk's foot leaves the cliff edge, Len pulls out a giant bear trap and places it where Jenk is due to land. He falls dead centre, and the enormous metal jaws clamp down, splitting him in half. Len gives out a high-pitched, childish laugh, which is followed by a laughing track of very amused, sadistic children, before the credits start to roll. RIP.

Finally, Jav seems to venture back to World War II. He closes his eyes. He's shaking and sweating. He's a soldier, sitting on a bench in the middle of the battlefield. His forearms are covered in blood and Len, Jenk and I are lying dead on the muddy floor around the bench. Bombs are obliterating the ground around us and soldiers are running past, gas masks on.

A German soldier walks up to Jav and points the barrel of his gun at his forehead. "What are you doing, soldier?" he shouts at Jav. He orders him to fight, but he can't. He can't even move from the bench. The soldier grabs Jav's bloodied arms, his fingers digging into the wounds, and throws him onto the floor. The gun is once again pointed in his face and he can't stop shaking. He closes his eyes and hears a shot. Splatters of blood hit his face, his body tenses and he stops breathing. He hears his body thud to the floor and eases his eyes open as slowly as he can. Jav looks at the corpse now lying in front of him. He's lying on his stomach, but his head is facing sideways so Jav can see his lifeless, unblinking eyes, and they look so familiar.

I open my eyes and it seems as though those irrational visions smuggled their way out of my imagination and into reality.

"I proper need the toilet..." I say, waiting for confirmation on going for a wild wee.

"Go for a wild wee," Len confirms.

I will. I get up from the bench and walk into the forest. I find a flat patch of ground and look around. Next thing I know, I wake up, lying flat on my back, looking up at the clear, starry sky. I can't believe I passed out already.

I walk back to the bench laughing and I start to explain what just happened.

"Ayyy, whitey!" Jenk laughs.

"You whitied about five seconds ago," I retaliate.

All of a sudden, a large white rabbit hops out from behind a distant bush on the other side of the field. It takes giant, exaggerated hops towards us so that it is just a few feet away from the bench. It stares at me with big, red, emotionless, unblinking eyes and twitches its nose before taking another enormous leap to the row of bushes next to us. On the other side is a path that runs the entire length of the narrow park. I interrupt the group's entertainment to tell them a story.

"Guys, the other day, me and Laurie were out, and we saw a couple of white rabbits and I regret not following them when they hopped away. I need to follow this one." I stand up and offer everyone the option of coming with me onto the dusty path.

"Alright," Len says, and stands up to follow me towards the bushes.

Jav and Jenkies following shortly after.

As we walk upon the forest floor, following a giant white bunny through a dark, narrow corridor of bushes and trees, I decide to ask how everybody else is feeling.

"Everyone doing okay?"

"Yeah," Len mumbles quickly and in a low hush

"Yeah!" Jenk shouts, almost sounding aggressive in a way, but still excited.

Javan doesn't even bother to reply.

"Do you hear that?" Len asks, speaking a little bit louder now.

"Yeahh..." I whisper, straining my hearing.

It sounds like a car horn coming from the right of the path, a lot further down than we are, though.

"What is that?" Jenk ponders, looking into the sky for answers.

"It's screaming," Javan answers.

We all listen closer now.

The white rabbit turns to look at us with its great big, bulging, red eyes. It twitches its nose a few times before falling through the ground, leaving us to fend for ourselves. Suddenly, I'm brought back to reality. We're left alone in the darkness and the deafening silence, apart from the bloodcurdling screams, of course. I stop walking for a moment, trying to decide whether to just turn back and return to the bench, but before I can even propose the idea, Javan trudges past me, on a mission to locate the source of the screaming. None of us object to his actions, and willingly follow him up the path again. The screaming escalates in its intensity the closer we get and soon there's only a small group of trees between us and the horrific scene which must be playing out in the darkness behind them.

I take a step forward and peek around a tree.

The scene unravels from a giant psychedelic swirl and I see two people on the ground among the twigs and the green leaves that have fallen from the giant, overbearing trees, which seem to huddle around us, forcing us to watch whatever is happening. At what feels like an immense speed, my vision zooms into the pair struggling on the floor. Ollie is standing over someone I can barely see from behind the small bush which is obstructing my view. His arm keeps flying up into the air and crashing back down towards the person on the ground, causing another burst of agonised screams.

I take a step forward, somehow not worried about the consequences of my actions, in order to see who is lying, half dead, behind the bush. I look down and see a human-sized banana wearing a monocle and a black top hat. It's screaming through a forced and painful-looking smile whilst Ollie continuously stabs a knife into the side of it, as thick, crimson blood pours out of the gashes. Its dark pupils slowly move sideways across its big, wide, white eyeballs, in the manner of an evil ventriloquist's dummy, and as soon as its eyes lock onto mine, the loudest thing I have ever heard comes out from between its clenched teeth. The words, "WOULD YOU BELIEVE?" rattle through my skull, causing me to cover my ears and fall to my knees in pain.

Meanwhile, Len's curiosity has been piqued, despite the screaming being almost too much for him to handle. He sees me collapse to the ground, clutching my head and rushes over to me and tries to ask me what I saw, but I can't seem to hear him. Needing to see for himself, he stays crouched down low and leans forward to look around the tree. He sees himself leaning over Ryan and stabbing him in the side of his stomach as Ryan screams and begs for Len to stop, but Len doesn't stop, he just keeps stabbing him, each time with more force then before.

Len is powerless to do anything other than watch himself committing a heinous crime, even though inside he is shouting at himself to stop, but his eyes and his mind feel as though they have been taken hostage by his body. Claustrophobia and helplessness paralyse him, as he watches himself continue to stab the innocent boy, as more and more blood pools around his body, seeping into the dry soil beneath him. Suddenly, a giant flower rises from the ground next to him. It's a red rose and it's dripping with Ryan's blood. The blood that is now all over Len's hands.

Simultaneously, the drugs are having an altogether different effect on Jenk. He feels amazing. Everything looks like a cartoon, everything down to the tiniest speck of dirt on his shoes. Even the screaming can't put him off having a good time. With everyone looking at what's going on, he strolls over to the patch of land surrounded by trees where all the commotion is coming from. A six-foot-high, black, jagged cat is standing over the tiny body of a brown, motionless mouse with giant ears. The mouse is attached to four trees by four separate sections of rope, tied around his limbs, each being stretched to unimaginable lengths. The cat suddenly pulls a giant Samurai sword out from behind his back. He holds it up in the air above the mouse's right leg and says something to the mouse in a language Jenk doesn't recognise. The cat looks at Jenk with darting eyes and smiles, showing off his feline grin, then he swings the sword down, severing the mouse's leg with a single stroke.

No blood comes out when the small, cubic limb gently falls to the floor, though, and a chorus of children begin to laugh all around us. The cat proceeds to slice off every one of the mouse's remaining limbs before vigorously stabbing him in the side of the stomach over and over again, until the small rodent becomes almost unrecognizable.

The whole walk here, Jav's not been able to get the image of that German soldier's scar-covered face and his gun pointing directly at him, out of his head. He can't help but notice the similarities between the soldier and Gaz. He's paranoid that he is going to get killed and he really doesn't want to find out where this screaming is coming from, but he still needs to see what's going on. He stands behind the group and looks on from a distance, hiding himself in the shadow of a large tree hunching over his back. The German soldier is standing over a young British boy. They both look at Jav, the boy with pleading, crying eyes, one with a giant gash running above it, through his eyebrow. And the German, with icy, bright, blue eyes shouts, "Die!" and smiles at Jav as he stabs the boy in the side of the stomach and the boy screams out in pain again. Jav falls backwards against the tree and starts to cry silently as the trees close in on him.

My hearing comes back to me and I notice Len crouched next to me with his arm around my shoulders. I look around at everybody and they all look just as worse for wear as I feel.

"We should go," I say quickly, and we all run back through the pitch black to the direction of the car park. We all clamber into my car and I lock the doors.

"Did you all see that...?" Jenk questions, probably because he thinks he just hallucinated the whole thing.

"Yeah..." I unfortunately reply, and so do Len and Jav.

I can hardly talk as I'm trying to process everything I've just seen. If that was Ollie, why didn't he kill us instead? And why the hell did I see a giant banana that looked like Bucket? The whole situation just doesn't make sense to me. Did it even happen? Maybe we all just had a bad trip and saw something that wasn't even there. I've never experienced anything like that before and I hope I never do again.

Len is wondering if he just killed Ryan? But how could that be possible? He watched himself do it! He knows he can't tell anybody about this, not even me! But he wonders if we saw him do it? He feels like he can't breathe; his heart is sinking to his stomach then pushes down hard in his chest when it finally comes back up. He can't stop fidgeting and the silence is making him so paranoid that the rest of us know that he's a murderer.

Jenk, too, is wondering what the hell he has just

seen? It was almost exactly the same as his other hallucination on the bench, so it must have just been another one. But then, what did everybody else see to react in the way they did? Wow... shrooms really aren't what he thought they were going to be. He feels like shit. No finesse, just stress.

Jav can't describe how he's feeling. It's like all his worst fears are coming true. He feels alone and depressed, even more so than he did before. He's hated every second of this trip and he can't wait for it to end. He feels as though he wants it to end now, right now. But how can he stop it? Maybe he should do what the German soldier told him to do when he saw him in the woods.

"Are we still going to sleep in the tent?" I break the silence.

"I can't go home," Len insists.

We bundle the tent out of the boot and pitch it up on a patch of grass far away from where we saw the murder. We crawl into the four-man tent and lie silently for a few moments.

Out of the silence, someone whispers with a quivering, scared voice, "I love you guys."

It is the most intense thing I've ever heard.

ONE DAY LATER:
THE INVESTIGATION BEGINS

W e pack up the tent and get into the car within fifteen minutes of waking up. Nobody says a word. It's like every one of us is living a completely different life, alone, but doing the exact same thing together.

Once in the car, nobody wants to go anywhere. The silence cannot be broken by the sound of a car engine.

"Let's walk," I say, as I'm already halfway out of the car.

They get back out, too and walk alongside me. I decide to walk the opposite way, across the nature trail, the one closest to the car. We stop in a field of sheep where we've smoked before and sit along the rickety wooden fence, in silence.

"Are we going to talk about last night?" Jav puts the feelers out.

"No," Len replies, looking as if he's about to throw up.

So we don't talk about it. We don't talk at all, in fact.

We walk back, starting towards the main road, planning on walking home. I'll pick up my car tomorrow.

Before we even get to the junction at the end of the road, a police car pulls up next to us and Len stops dead in his tracks. I turn around and look at him. He looks like he's trying to find a quick escape route, so I walk over to him and hold his hand. I look him in the eyes, without saying a word, and he calms down, but his eyes are still full of fear.

A male police officer with a stocky build and a bald head steps out of the driver's side, followed shortly by a smaller woman with long brown hair who emerges from the passenger side. Both are in police uniforms with high-vis vests over the top. They begin to walk towards us, the man sending a message through his walkie-talkie before shouting over to us.

"Is that one of your cars?" he asks, pointing to my car, parked up not far behind us.

"Yeah, it's mine," I shout back.

"I'd like to ask you all a few questions, please."
He approaches, looking very serious, stopping about a
foot away from us while the policewoman stays by
the car.

"Okay. About what?" I enquire.

"The events of last night. We checked the park's
CCTV footage and saw your car pulling into the car
park last night. A few hours later, a brutal murder
took place further into the forest. Where were you?"

It was real. We didn't hallucinate it.

I put my hand over my mouth and feel
unbelievably light-headed.

Javan falls to his knees with his head in his hands.
Len starts to shake and rubs his hand back and forth
over his hair. Jenk just stands there and looks
perplexed, along with the police officer who now
suspects us of murder.

"Shall we take a ride to the station?" he insists, in
a very grave voice.

I take a deep breath and say there's no need,
before I explain our story.

"We were sitting on the bench over there, having
a cigarette after work. We thought we could hear
rustling in the forest but put it down to the rabbits
that are always hopping around at this time of year
and we just lost track of time, so we decided to pitch
the tent I keep in my boot, because I felt too tired to
drive us all home. We went for a little walk in the

opposite direction this morning and then we started speaking to you."

"So why did you all react like that if you had nothing to do with it?" he questions.

"We were joking about what the noises could be all night. We feel terrible about it now. Check the CCTV again, you'll see we're telling the truth," Jenk jumps in nicely.

"We wish we could tell you more," I finish off.

He takes our names and phone numbers and says he'll be in touch again soon, then both police officers get back into the patrol car and drive off.

"I'll drive us all home, come on," I state, and we all turn around and walk back to the car.

I turn up for work at 7 o'clock and I'm still speechless. I plaster a pathetic attempt at a smile onto my face and hope that it repels any questions from regulars. As if my night couldn't be worse, Francis is seated at the bar with his wife and Phillip and the rest of that group are sitting at the table in front of the bar again. I don't say hello to anybody at the bar, I just lean on the machine that cleans the glasses and stare at one of the pictures on the wall.

"Penny for 'em," I hear someone next to me say.

I look up and see Philip standing at the bar,

leaning towards me. I look into his eyes, matching his icy glare before giving out a small laugh without even smiling.

"What can I get you?" I ask him.

"Nothing, I just came over to talk to you," he states.

"Oh right... about what?"

"Anything. What did you get up to last night?" He takes a swig from his pint without taking his eyes away from mine as he says it.

"Not much. Just stayed in with some mates. What did you do?" I ask him in return.

"I was on a date!" he smirks.

"Oh yeah? Does that mean you won't be asking me out anymore then?" I joke, hoping that the answer is yes.

"Well... if you want to go on a date with me..." He winks.

"I'm alright, actually," I reply, wiping the smile from his face. His new expression resonates a faint hint of ferocity at having been rejected.

I get ready to confront him about following me and Jav the other day, but someone on the other side of the bar is waiting to be served so I walk off without saying another word and Philip goes and sits back down.

Strangely, Francis is being extremely kind to me tonight. He jokes with me about the struggles of wearing glasses and he doesn't once complain about my terrible bartending skills, which puts me in a somewhat better mood.

The shift goes quickly from then on and once I'm in my car, I check my phone and I find a text from Len: *Hi. Can you come over?*

Obviously, I say yes, and set off straight away. I pull up onto the kerb outside his house and before I even get out of the car, he's standing in the arch of his front door, waiting for me.

He looks almost godlike with his shiny, blond hair curling lightly over his forehead and the dim light shining out from behind him. I walk up to the door and he steps aside to let me in. The house is warm and bustling with noise from the kitchen and the front room. We walk into his bedroom which is right next to the front door and I sit down on the bed.

"Are you alright?" I ask, as I watch him pacing up and down his room.

"I can't handle it, Flic!" he panics.

"I know. We shouldn't have lied to the police like that," I admit.

But that's not what he's referring to. "No, Flic. It's not that."

He shakes his head and sits down next to me. He's intertwining his fingers together vigorously and his knee is shaking quicker than it's ever done before, sending a constant vibration through the bed and deep into my bones.

"What is it then?" I ask with concern, putting my hand on his knee.

"I killed Ryan!" he shouts, before putting his head in his hands and shaking uncontrollably.

"Len, what are you on about?" I'm convinced it couldn't have been him but, from the way he reacted, I'm becoming unsure.

"I saw it. I saw myself stabbing Ryan."

"How could you have seen yourself?"

"I was watching!"

"You were hallucinating," I try to reassure him, even more so by stroking his knee.

He looks at me with sad eyes swimming in tears. "So... it wasn't real?" he asks.

"Sadly, I think it *was* real... but I saw Ollie, not you."

"Ollie..." he ponders, trying to remember who that is. "Oh shit, I completely forgot about him! It has to be him. He was so dodgy in college!" he recalls.

"Well yeah, but I don't know if I can believe everything I saw."

"What do you mean?" he asks.

"You saw Ryan being murdered. I saw a giant banana that looked like Julian Bucket..." I explain slowly.

We look at each other for a while before a little smile starts to form on his face, forcing me to reciprocate. Soon enough, we're both rolling around on the bed crying with laughter.

He asks me if I'll stay over with him tonight and I agree, mainly because I feel like I just need the company of someone who understands what I've got to deal with right now. We watch a TV series together cuddled up in bed, before falling asleep.

FIVE DAYS LATER:

AMSTERDAM

I t's our last day in college, ever! I turn up in high spirits as I walk with Jenkies to our media lesson. On our travels through the long corridor, we spot Ciggsy walking out of another corridor on the right. He sees us and joins us on our wander.

"Reckon Ollie will be in today?" he asks.

"Defo, but he'll be late again, and Gilbert won't be very happy," I reply.

"I love Ollie," Ciggsy declares, hopefully joking.

We get into the classroom and sit down in our usual seats next to each other.

Our teacher, Gilbert, walks in and talks about what we're going to cover today. In the middle of her very informative speech, Ollie opens the classroom door and attempts to walk to his seat, which is unfortunately adjacent to mine.

"Why are you late?" Gilbert frowns in annoyance.

"Redecorating," Ollie whispers in his slightly cracked, high-pitched, eerie voice, speaking to Gilbert from beneath his brow bones.

Gilbert just looks at him, slightly terrified, and says no more.

Me, Jenk and Ciggsy are all desperately trying not to laugh at him and his insane excuse for being late, as he creeps over to the table and sits down, looking at all three of us, trying to kill us with his eyes.

The lesson begins and we're free to talk amongst ourselves whilst we work.

We're talking about everyone in our class and I can see that Ollie is pretending not to be listening to us, but he clearly is.

"I love looking at all these beautiful faces! Includinggg... Ollie. I'm scared." Ciggsy is soon cut off from his joke as Ollie immediately looks up at us at the first mention of his name.

I can't hold in the laughter, though, and my eyes start streaming with tears. Jenk has covered his face with his hand and is silently laughing to himself, but you can still see his shoulders juddering up and down, and Ciggsy is staring at his laptop screen with wide eyes and a 'that was funny but now I'm in danger' look on his face.

Once Ollie looks away, Ciggsy whispers to us

both, "Did you see him reaching for his bag then? He was one hundred percent about to shoot up the class!"

Despite Ciggsy taking pictures of Ollie and us three laughing about him right in front of his face, we manage to make it out of the lesson alive and we walk to the car park together.

We take a short cut through a tiny mud path and we see Ollie a few paces in front of us. Ciggsy starts saying his name, getting louder every time, to see if he turns around, which he does, simultaneously throwing us an evil glare. We finally get off the path and we're about to cross the road, with Ollie standing not too far away still, when Jenk has an epiphany.

"We're never going to see Ollie again!" he shouts, as the realisation pops into his head.

Ollie turns and looks again, and we run across the road laughing and screaming in pretend terror.

We get home for a matter of minutes before grabbing our suitcases and heading for the airport. We get there and go straight to the bar, buying a pint each and sitting down at a small table to watch last night's World Cup highlights. I get halfway through my drink when I look up at the departure board and see our flight with the words *GATES CLOSING* highlighted by a panicked bright red colour. I tell everyone that the gate is closing but they're in denial; surely not, we only just got here? But once they turn and see the board themselves, we all down the rest of our drinks and sprint through the terminals to our gate.

In the distance, we see a small man holding a piece of paper at the boarding desk. "Are you going to Amsterdam?" he shouts over to us, and the group of lads walking in front of us.

"Yeah!" everybody shouts back, Javan punching the air and doing a three-sixty spin.

"Alright, mate, calm down," I laugh, but it's only him that doesn't find it funny.

I sit next to Jav on the plane and I watch him play a football-related game on his phone whilst simultaneously talking about football.

Jenkies tells us that his sister came here a few weeks before and got charged two hundred euros for a taxi from the airport and so we decide that we will be extra careful with our transport choices when we get there.

This idea swiftly flies out the window because, as soon as we step through the automatic doors at the airport into the midsummer heat, a man holding a taxi sign runs over to us and pretty much kidnaps us, leading us into a multi-storey car park. Once in the car, he has a very heated phone conversation with his wife in a different language.

"This. Is going to be. So. Expensive," Len whispers to me from the side of his mouth.

I just look at him and laugh.

"Sorry about that, guys. Wives, you know," the taxi driver says.

And we all just nod and laugh as if we did know.

"You guys ever been here before?" he asks us.

"Nah, first time," Jenk replies.

"Right, so," he begins, "you don't want to be going to any of these tourist places like The Bulldogs. They're famous, yes, but the weed is shit, makes you sleepy, *ja?* I'll take you to one of my favourites, the weed is good there." And so that's where we get off – a tropical-looking coffee shop with a tiny security desk at the front.

"That'll be sixty-five euros please, guys," he announces, once he's told us all the best weed to buy.

I look at Len and he pulls a face that means 'not bad', so we pay, and we get out.

Once at the desk, a man with tanned skin and dark hair asks to see our ID. We order our weed at that desk and walk inside.

The highlights from a different game are on the TV now and so we sit and watch them and discuss the upcoming England game against Croatia. This weed we're smoking is one hundred times better than anything we smoke back at home and we can definitely feel it. After one spliff I feel numb all over, but in a nice way. I look at Len who's sitting at the end of the table and he doesn't look healthy. His legs are shaking and he's constantly whipping his head around and looking at everybody.

"What's up?" I ask him.

"This doesn't feel right," he says, referring to smoking indoors sat next to strangers who are also smoking weed.

I tell him to come and sit next to me, which he does, and after the next spliff he finally chills out and he's slouched back in the chair, stroking a plastic leaf draping from a giant tropical plant in the corner next to us.

"Why are you stroking that leaf?" I ask, confused but amused.

"I dunno, I can't help it," he says and swiftly lets go of the leaf.

After literally a minute, we're mid-conversation and I see his hand slowly rise up to his shoulder where the leaf is hanging, and he begins to stroke it again.

"You're stroking it again!" I point out to him.

He looks at his hand and whips it away from the leaf again, as if he's scared of it. Perhaps it did have a life of its own.

We finish up in the café and get a taxi to the hotel. We order room service, play cards and smoke weed until the early hours. Me and Len walk back to our room and it's boiling hot. Our room doesn't have a fan and so we just leave the window open to let some cool air in, but it doesn't really help that much, anyway.

The next morning, after a long discussion, we decide that we should try shrooms again and see if it goes better than last time; well, it definitely can't be worse. But first we decide to go to the sex museum and the Frank house and so we buy a few spliffs to take with us. We smoke one and walk into the museum. Whilst waiting in line, we hear the blaring audio of some very intense lovemaking that we have to shout over in order to buy our tickets. There are pictures of weird sex all over the place and we spend the whole time making dick jokes and laughing at the slightest thing. We're 'in and out' within ten minutes and we start walking down the canal towards Anne's house, smoking a couple more spliffs and wolfing down a space cake on the way. Once we get there, we stand on the pavement across the road and stare up at the tall terraced house, taking in all the harrowing history of the place.

After a couple of questionable comments, we realise that we aren't really in the right state of mind for this so we decide instead to head over to the magic shroom shop and buy the highest strength truffles, then take them back to the hotel.

We're all extremely apprehensive about taking

them, because of what happened last time, but nobody has said anything since.

"I don't know if I want to do it," Javan quivers.

"Come on, Jav, we'll be fine. Nothing bad can happen here, we're in a locked room and we're all in a good mood. Just relax," I try to convince him.

It works, and he decides that he will, despite still not wanting to.

We turn on the TV and flick through the foreign channels before we cheers a shroom, as if they were drinks, and start chewing them. Followed by more and more.

We decide to play Uno whilst we wait for them to kick in. Jav's on Uno and Jenkies puts down a pick up four card for him. He throws his last card down and shouts, "I hate this game!" We all laugh out of shock and I ask him what's wrong.

"We're acting as if it never happened, we haven't even spoken about it since! I can't deal with this on my own!" he shouts.

"Jav, calm down! We haven't spoken about it because we didn't even see it actually happen," Len replies, sounding very nervous.

"Don't put us in a bad mood, Jav, we want to enjoy this trip," Jenk insists.

Jav gets up off the bed and storms into the bathroom, shutting the door behind him.

We all look at each other and roll our eyes, smirking slightly as we do so.

"I've got an idea," Jenk says with a smile.

He gets up and walks over to the wall with the bathroom switch on it and he turns it off.

We all sit in silence in anticipation of a shout of rage, or anything at all. But we don't hear a peep. After a minute or so we begin to worry and shout his name. The door slowly creaks open and in a low, hushed voice he says to us, "Come in here, now."

We all look at each other, puzzled, but step into the tiny square bathroom anyway. Light from our room floods into the darkened bathroom to reveal Jav perched on the toilet seat lid. Jenk sits on the sink so I sit on one of Jav's knees and Len stands next to the door, which he's told to close.

"Welcome to the Ket Hole..." Jav announces mysteriously.

We observe in complete silence and complete darkness until Len shouts out in amazement. I start to look around the blackness and suddenly, in extreme detail, down to every strand of hair, the white outlines of a team of horses gallop straight past me. For some reason the shrooms are making me want to scratch and bite constantly, and so, without realising, I'm vigorously clawing at Javan's knee, but we're all too distracted for either of us to notice. After about ten minutes of sitting in the darkness shouting *"Whoa!"* at all the incredible hallucinations we're seeing, Jenk opens the door, filling the bathroom once again with a bright yellow light, bringing us all back to reality as our hallucinations disappear under the rays of the dazzling sunlight streaming in through the bedroom windows. What once was a beautiful vision of majestic horses with their glistening manes gracefully floating through the wind, is now a tiny shower with no curtain or door and white walls all around.

We walk back into the bedroom and lie back down on the bed.

"We should go outside, there's a park about twenty minutes away." Say no more, Jenkies.

We get our stuff together in under ten seconds, including the mini football Len bought earlier this morning, and we head straight out the front entrance of the hotel. I have with me a two-litre bottle of water, which I've already started scratching the bottom of.

We get two minutes down the road before we stop and sit on the edge of the canal, watching the bridge rise to allow a cargo ship to pass through and we are so entranced that we stay there for half an hour just watching our feet hang over the swishing murky water below, eating some more shrooms whilst we have the chance.

"Shall we keep going?" Jav asks and we all agree that we should.

We take about thirty steps further down the road before we spot a big metal electrical box and end up doing nothing but standing around it in awe for another considerable amount of time.

We turn the corner and spot a small children's playground in front of a long row of terraced apartments. We run over and start to climb on all the equipment. I play hopscotch on a grid of squares which have clearly been drawn on the ground by some children. Once I get all the way to the end, feeling the most energetic I have in years despite my illness, I look up and see a ginger tabby cat with a blue bandana around its neck. I walk closer to it and put my hand out to stroke it, but it runs away. By now, we've been here for another half an hour and so Jav says we should move on again. I start to walk away and as soon as I get in front of Jenk, he holds his hand up to signal us to stop.

"Wait!" Jenk approaches the cat, looking it in the eyes, the cat looking back, almost as if it's in a trance. He keeps his hand in the same position as he begins to slowly creep closer to the cat. They're looking into each other's eyes like they know the other's deepest, darkest secrets and the cat starts to mimic Jenk's movements. We stand there at a distance, watching in disbelief as he charms the tabby. He moves closer to it, bends down and strokes it once from head to tail.

"*Whaaaaaat!*" I shout, partly out of amazement and partly because I'm jealous that the cat didn't let me stroke it.

Jenk looks at me and says "come," signaling me to do so with his hand gesture, too. I walk over and the cat allows me to stroke it. It feels so soft and I can feel every individual hair gliding across my cold hand.

"Come on, Doctor Donothing, the park's supposed to be twenty minutes away and we've been out for almost two hours now," Jav shouts over to us.

"Just enjoy yourself, Jav. Do you not feel anything?" I ask him.

"I do, but I just want to keep going." And he turns away immediately.

If I wasn't on shrooms, Jav's attitude would have probably annoyed me, but instead I laugh and follow on.

We take a shortcut behind a petrol station and it leads us on to an abandoned train track and some run-down-looking mechanics and other odd shops. As we're walking along, a massive, mangled bird flies down and perches itself on a wooden bollard on the other side of the tracks to us.

"Bet I can tame that bird," Jenk challenges.

"You definitely can! I believe in you!" I egg him on.

The bird must have heard us because it snaps its ruffled grey head in our direction, its little beady eyes scanning over every one of us individually.

Jenk walks up to it slowly, looking it in the eye, as he did with the cat. The bird looks straight ahead but keeps an intense side eye on Jenk and his every move.

"Go on, Jenkies, I want to see this happen!" Len joins in.

We watch and wait for him to make a move, but a group of joggers come bounding past and it startles the bird, so Jenk takes a step back from it. But soon enough, however, he's ready to approach it again and, after a while of carefully biding his time, he sweeps the back of his hand elegantly across the length of the bird's wing.

I start howling with laughter at how amazing it is that he can tame any animal he wants, but I'm soon stunned silent as the bird tries to peck at his hand with its long black beak. We all scream and laugh and run away a little bit further down the tracks.

"You've one hundred percent got rabies now, Jenkies," I say.

"Yeah, that bird was minging, don't touch me," Len follows on and we all laugh.

We don't have to walk very far before we find something else that we can play with in the form of a pile of giant metal pipes stacked on top of each other, forming a pyramid shape. Two of us stand on either side and pull faces at each other through the holes in the middle. Len throws the ball down one side and Jenk catches it at the other end before throwing it back through to our side again.

"Let me have a go!" Len passes me the ball and I take a step backwards.

I throw the tiny ball with reasonable force and somehow it misses every single hole and bounces back towards me and hits me in the shoulder. I let out a quick *"AH!"* and run after the ball. I pick it up and throw it towards the pipes again. For the second time, it bounces straight back and hits me in the other shoulder, so I throw myself backwards dramatically and I can't stop laughing.

"Flic, there's about nine giant holes, how are you missing them all?" Len condescends and comes over to take the ball from me.

"One more go!" I demand.

I walk up to the pipes and slam-dunk the ball into one of the higher pipes and Jenk catches it at the other end. He tells us he's going to throw it into the very top pipe, which he does, and so me and Len wait for the ball to drop out of the end, but it never does. Me and Len look at each other, and then we look at Jav and Jenk through the pipes.

"Oh shit," Len utters.

But not to worry, Jav to the rescue. He launches a water bottle into the pipe, sending both items flying out towards me and Len.

We decide to keep walking to reduce the chances of us losing the ball again. As we strut through the derelict cowboy town, we're all just doing our own thing, looking around at everything we can possibly look at. I walk over to Jenk, who's staring at a wall and laughing. I look at the giant piece of blue metal which has his attention, but see nothing there.

"What are you laughing at?" I ask him.

"Just this wall." He laughs, shrugs and shakes his

head.

We finally make it to the park, but we carry on walking because, in the distance, we see a famous football stadium and we know that there is a small football pitch next to it, named after one of the greatest footballers in history. We get there and it's just as good as we expected. We have a whale of a time taking penalties against each other, but after an hour I get bored and decide to take a closer look at the stadium. I look up at the waving flags and the gigantic floodlights peering from behind the intimidating coliseum walls and I think about all the amazing memories people have had here, all the tears of joy and, of course, of sadness. I can hear the crowds cheering and chanting the names of their star players. I feel the vibrations of the euphoria all around me, lingering in the air from years gone by.

I don't know how long I'm standing there for but, when I turn back around to look at the pitch, I can hardly see the lads through the darkness of the night which seems to have crept up on us very suddenly. There's a statue of Johan Cruyff and another footballer outside the stadium. It pinpoints the moment the Netherlands were given a penalty in the first minute of the 1974 World Cup against West Germany. It's made out of pieces of metal that look like they've been stuck together and flattened. I feel the need to grab hold of one of his wrists, like it's really him and this is a once in a lifetime opportunity, so I do, but it's freezing cold, so I quickly let go. I stand in front of the statue and look into the face of the metal athlete. Soon, though, it starts to creep me out because it looks like a big metal man running right for me. Len comes up behind me and gives me a hug, asking what I'm doing over here on my own. I tell him what I've been looking at and we talk about the statue.

"Do you remember that film with the argonauts and there's that big statue that comes to life and tries to kill them all?" I ask.

"Never seen that," he laughs, probably because I've described the most ridiculous sounding part of the film.

So, I start to describe the scene where the giant statue tries to kill all of Jason's argonauts, accompanying my tale with childish demonstrations. I look up at him whilst I bring my animated description to a close and he's standing there contemplatively smiling at me, as if he's proud to be in this moment with me.

"What?" I ask shyly.

He pulls me towards him and gives me a hug and I smile to myself while I rest my head on his muscular chest. We stand in silence for a moment, just enjoying being together and being so close to each other.

"Flic..." He pushes my shoulders away from him a little, to make me look at him.

"Yeah?" I lift my head up and stare into his soft, crystal blue eyes.

"I love you so much, you know. It's weird, I've never felt like this before... I really want you as my girlfriend, Flic."

I manage to look at him for a few more seconds before becoming overwhelmed by every emotion that ever existed, so I quickly put my head back onto his chest as I try and hold back my tears. I can't help but cry, though, because in this moment I'm struck by the fierce realisation that I feel exactly the same way, too, and it is a realisation made all the more powerful and heartbreaking by knowing that we will only be together for a few more months.

"If I wasn't on shrooms, I'd cry, too," he says, and we both have a little laugh, as he wipes away the tears from my cheeks.

I look down at the floor as he strokes my hair, and I decide that I have to tell him – it's now or never. "I can't be your girlfriend, Len."

"Why not?" His face drops into a frown.

"It's not because I don't want to be, I really do. But I'm not going to be around much longer," I explain, trying to soften the blow, but he doesn't get it.

"What do you mean?" he asks, and so I explain without censoring anything.

He listens in silence and it tears me apart to see the look on his face. I tell him about when I first noticed the symptoms and the first diagnosis. I can see that he can't understand how he didn't know any of this before.

"So, there's nothing they can do now that I've refused chemo, they think I won't make it to next year," I conclude.

He just stands and looks down at me, scanning my face to make sure I'm not playing some sort of cruel trick on him. He doesn't say anything for the longest time.

"I still want you to be my girl though, Flic. I love you. I don't want anybody else," he says, looking deep into my eyes, his thumb rubbing my cheek.

This sets me off crying again, but this time I smile and nod my head.

"Let's have the best year. Together," I say, and I hold his big, soft hands in mine and squeeze them tightly.

He leans forward and gently kisses me on my forehead.

(He later tells me that this was one of the best moments of his life, despite the horrible news, and even now, just thinking about the honesty behind his words that night makes me smile.)

We walk back to the pitch where Jenk and Jav are still kicking the ball around. Jav looks at me with big, sad eyes before turning back around to continue playing. I sit on the sideline and watch the three of them pass it around to each other and take shots at the goal, trying to show off to each other how skillful they are. The ball hurtles towards Jenkies and he kicks it way too hard so that it flies over the tall, green mesh fence and rolls down the bank on the other side and then splashes into the canal behind the pitch. For a few seconds we say nothing, we just look at each other, and the canal, with open mouths, Jav with his hands on his head in disbelief.

"*Nooo*, that can't happen!" he shouts.

As I sit there and watch them walk over to the canal one by one, I get the feeling that we've not seen the last of that ball yet.

"We'll get it back," I say to them, but I don't think they hear me.

I watch them for a minute before going back to playing a game on my phone. Not long after, I hear someone shout, "Yes, Jav!" from behind me. I turn my head and see Javan appear from behind the grassy banks of the canal, clutching the wet football in his hands. I smirk smugly to myself, having known all along that we were going to get the ball back.

They continue to play football for another hour, eating the last of the shrooms in between shots, but it soon becomes darker and colder, and the seedy characters start to emerge from the shadows, so we decide to walk back.

On the way to the park we'd had Jenk leading us

via Google Maps, but as we start walking back, we realise that we don't need a map because we've remembered stopping and looking at everything that we're now crossing paths with again. On the walk, Len asks for a drink of water from the bottle that I've been holding all day. I pass it to him, and he notices the bottom of the bottle, which is now completely circular rather than flat and square.

It's two o'clock in the morning by the time we get back to the hotel, the walk having taken us only twenty minutes this time. We go back up to the rooms, Len and I planning on joining Jenk and Jav in their room after we've had a shower and changed into something comfier. As we're sitting on the bed, we hear a tiny buzzing noise and see a mosquito flying around the room. I watch it fly higher and higher until it lands on the ceiling, revealing hundreds more mosquitoes which have snuck in through our open window and made a home on our bedroom ceiling.

"We can't sleep in here," I say, and Len agrees.

We walk next door to Jav and Jenk's room and once we're there, all we do is eat, since we haven't had any food all day apart from breakfast, because you're not supposed to eat whilst on shrooms. We stay up for another hour, talking and laughing about our day and how we never want it to end, and so we go down to the lobby, smoke another spliff and play pool, pairing up to create two teams, me and Len, Jav and Jenk. The lads storm into the lead, with only one ball left before they're on the black; me and Len still have three more to pot before we get to that stage, Jenk thanking his snooker champion dad, Tone, for his inherited pool playing abilities.

I step up to the mark, feeling more confident than ever after being jeered by the opposition. I concentrate hard, lining up my shot and pulling back the cue while the hotel lobby falls silent in anticipation. The contact between the white and the cue is perfect, sinking the blue striped ball into the top right pocket. I walk down to that end of the table and line up my next shot, and I've set myself up, making my job extra easy. Another stripe rolls down into the chamber on the side of the pool table. One ball left. I look at Len and he smiles, 'go on'. I look back at the white ball and line up my shot again. It hits the cushion right next to the pocket and I straighten up, thinking it's all over, but the ball bounces back into another pocket.

"WAHEYYY!" I celebrate, making the hotel receptionists behind the check-in desk look up from their computers. Len is willing me to succeed and it makes me really want to pot the black first time, but I miss as it hits the cushion and sets Jenk up for his final shot. I shake my head and walk over to Len. He puts his arm around my shoulder and tells me that I did really well. Jenk pots his final spot and so their team joins us on the black. It's a tense moment for all four of us. Javan wipes his sweaty brow with the towel he brought down from the room, and Jenk bottles it under the pressure, missing the easiest shot of the game.

"Tone would not be vereh appeh with you, Jenkies!" me and Len taunt in Manchester accents, despite Tone not even having one himself.

Team 'Flen' end up winning the game, as well as the next two, so it's fair to say that we are the undisputed pool champions of the holiday.

We go and sit outside in the smoking area at the front entrance of the hotel and we smoke all our remaining spliffs. After we smoke the first, Len and I head back inside to go to the toilet. On our way there, we spot a leaflet on the side of the bar for 24/7 pizza delivery and our brains work in alliance to tell the lads about our beautiful discovery. We order two large pizzas and a side of chicken nuggets, and we only have to wait around forty-five minutes for the delivery man to arrive, after which we take the food upstairs to our room.

As we sit there, eating pizza, laughing and watching funny cartoons on the small TV, I take a second to look at us all together and really appreciate the moment and the love I have for my three best friends.

This is what taking shrooms is supposed to feel like.

. . .

I wake up lying sideways on the foot of two single beds pushed together. Cold air from the small, rotating desk fan, left on overnight, blows into my face, prompting me to wake up properly. I look around. Len is lying next to me, sound asleep, his face scrunched up against the pillow and the slightest flow of dribble running out of his mouth. There's a small gap in between him and Javan, who's also asleep, but has fallen into the crack in the middle of the bed, and so his body is pretty much folded in half. I have a silent laugh to myself before wondering where Jenk is.

The bathroom door is closed and so I reckon he's in there and place my head back down on the pillow. After about ten minutes, there's still no sign of Jenkies, so I sit up in bed and instantly I see his long, scrawny legs sprawled out on the floor. Is he dead? Has he fallen and knocked himself out? I lean over further to look at his face and his eyes are closed, his mouth is open and he's lightly snoring. I smile and lie back down again, content with the fact that none of my friends are dead. Len stirs in his sleep and he puts his arm over my stomach. He opens one of his eyes slightly and I smile at him. He smiles back and kisses me on the cheek before closing his eye again and resting his chin on my shoulder.

. . .

We get dressed and order a taxi to take us into the city centre. We get into the car and the driver is an old Dutchman in a suit, with a toothpick in his mouth. The car is very nice inside and we openly express to him our love for the white leather seats and the brown tortoiseshell dashboard.

"Where you like me to take you, to centre?" he asks, in his strong but soothing accent.

Initially we say "Anywhere," but then decide on going back to Anne's house so that we know our way to the coffee shop from there, before heading to another museum. The driver nods and looks at us through the rear-view mirror as he begins to set off for Anne's place. It doesn't take that long to get there. We get out of the car and thank our driver, giving him a five out of five-star rating, then we walk to the nearest coffee shop.

"I don't feel like smoking today, I'm just going to do shrooms again," Jav states.

I question his decision, and the other three of us know that they won't have any effect on him so soon after taking the last lot, but he won't be swayed. We go back to the magic mushroom shop and he buys the same ones we took yesterday. We all cross over the road and enter a coffee shop that looks more like an Indian restaurant, and we buy some weed and sit down inside to smoke it. The three of us smoke it and pass it around to each other as we laugh about stories from yesterday. I have a quick look at Jav, who's not said a word since we sat down. He's eaten a few truffles by this point, but he says he doesn't feel anything yet. He's sat scrolling through social media sites on his phone with a sodden look on his face, so I ask if he's alright and he just nods 'yes' at me with a face that says otherwise, but I decide not to interrogate him anymore.

We walk to the next museum, which is all about the weird and wonderful things in life. We pay twenty euros for a ticket in a ticket office we spot on the way, but once we get there, we stroll through, no problem, without needing a ticket at all.

We get to one section of the museum that's all about space and we approach a small walkway leading to a bridge inside a tunnel, and the inner walls of this tunnel are spiraling and spinning around the bridge, throwing everybody off balance. Me, Jenk and Len, all stoned, are having the time of our lives, laughing and falling all over the place. Jav, however, is coolly waltzing down the middle of the bridge, without a smile or a wobble in sight; the shrooms aren't working for him at all.

We get out of the museum and everybody is laughing, apart from Jav and he doesn't want to be cheered up, so we just leave him to his own devices. Later, we order another taxi to take us back to the hotel. We're all really stoned by now, having stopped off for more weed after leaving the museum. We stand on the corner of a very busy main street with

127

multiple lanes, roads and traffic lights. The bike and the tram lanes have both been on a red light for a long time and so the traffic has built up considerably, so when Len spots our driver through the window of the tram, over the heads of multiple people on bikes, he points to the taxi and shouts, "It's him!", and all the people in the bike lane, and all the people on the tram, and all the people walking down the street, turn their heads and glare at us. Me and Jav walk away down the road whilst Len continues to stand on the spot and laugh in hysterics at his own stupidity.

We head over to our favourite coffee shop again to watch the England vs Croatia game. The Dutch guy behind the bar, who's been a dickhead every time we've met him, is, again, being a dickhead and taunting us, and two guys next to us, for being English. To make matters worse, we lose by one goal in extra time and Jav puts his forehead on the table and cries while we all sit there and look at each other, unaware of how to react, and unbothered because of how stoned we are.

In the taxi ride home, we can't help but make fun of Javan a bit for being so depressed about football. He has his earphones in and is ever so glumly looking out of the window at the dark sky.

"Bet he's got a slow version of *It's Coming Home*

on and he's pretending he's in the music video," I whisper, in case he can still hear me.

This sends Len into a fit of laughter and he begins to join in with the joke.

"Yeah and he gets home and goes straight to his fully England decorated room and cries into his Harry Kane pillow," he imagines.

This keeps going on for the entire fifteen-minute car journey home, Jenk in the front laughing and occasionally joining in with comments about Harry McGuire bed sheets and replica trophies he keeps in his room. We decide to have one more spliff when we get back to the hotel and go straight to bed, since it's our big day tomorrow, Tenacious Toes!

We get ready at 6 o'clock and get a taxi to the venue, a small renovated church with colourful stained glass windows above the stage. The lights dim and a spotlight comes onto the stage. Everyone is chanting for them to come out. After what seems like forever, one member of the band comes out on stage wearing nothing but a small pair of retro football shorts and his black handlebar moustache. He kicks a signed football into the crowd and everybody chants his name in chorus. The rest of the band join him on stage and the noise is immense.

Len puts his arm around my shoulder as soon as the first song begins to play, making me enjoy it even more. After a few songs, there's a short break whilst they get ready to play the next song.

The infamous Hawaiian guitar intro begins and all four of us look at each other and celebrate and we have a group hug; we all stand in line with our arms around each other as we listen to the song that reminds us most of us all being together.

Every song they play is incredible and, in the moment, I think to myself that I'll never ever forget this day, being in Amsterdam with my three best friends, listening to our favourite band live, without a care in the world and I will treasure this memory for as long as I live. Which tragically isn't going to be very long.

After the gig, we walk back to our coffee shop, which is conveniently just down the road, and smoke some more spliffs as we talk about our day. By this time, we're seven spliffs deep and we all feel extremely stoned. We sit on the wooden chairs outside the shop, looking out across the road, where there's a small, indie-looking bar with graffiti covering the walls at the entrance. As we sit there, we see a guy walk out of the bar with the same handlebar moustache and big curly afro as the band member, Freddy Krill.

"Is that Freddy Krabs?" Jav asks excitedly.

"Nah, it's just someone who looks like him. He's a BTEC Freddy, mate," Len replies, debunking Jav's dreams.

Not long after, we see him return with another guy with long ginger hair, wearing the same style of clothing as another member of the band.

"Wait... Is that Seamus?" I ask.

"Kind of looks like him... might just be another BTEC version," Len replies again, making us all laugh.

A man walks out of the coffee shop and asks if he can borrow our lighter. He starts a conversation with us and asks us what we've been up to in Amsterdam. We tell him about the gig we've just been to and how much we enjoyed it. He explains that he's an optician here in Dam and that he's sold sunglasses to, and is good friends with, the band.

"No way!" is all I can manage to say as he tells us insider knowledge about the personalities of the band members.

"Yes, they come here a lot, actually. They spend most of their time in that bar across the road," the optician tells us.

We all look at each other and laugh at our stupidity of calling the real people BTEC versions of themselves. We finish up the conversation and we make the rash decision to go into the bar with hopes of meeting them. The optician tells us that they don't deal well with people who act like fans, asking for pictures and bombarding them with questions, so naturally I am the one who's sent into the bar. I walk across the road and into the small building, and all five members are sat together, huddled into a small brown leather booth. Freddy gets up and walks over to the bar to get a drink, so I make my move. I stand next to him as he orders, and he looks at me from head to toe once over and then smiles at me, so I smile back and for a few seconds I don't say anything, trying to think of something witty to say.

"I like your moustache," I blurt out, forgetting what I'd thought about saying.

He laughs and says, "Cheers."

"What are you drinking?" I ask, trying to keep the conversation going as he waits for his drinks.

"Just a pint of Heins," he replies, with a smile and a nod.

"Can I buy it for you?" I ask, sounding more like I want to go back to his hotel room rather than meet his mates as well.

He shakes his head and says no, offering to buy me one instead, so obviously I let him.

"Come and sit with us," he says to me, passing me my drink.

I try to keep my cool and just shrug slightly and smile. "Okay!"

"I'm Freddy, by the way," he introduces himself.

"Nice to meet you, I'm Flic," I reply, as if I don't already know who Freddy Krabs is!

We get to the booth and he gets everybody's attention.

"Guys, this is Flic. She offered to buy me a drink

so it's the least I can do." He laughs, and the rest of the band laugh with him.

They go around the group and introduce themselves to me. I sit down on the end of the booth next to Freddy and chat to the band.

Seamus leans over and asks me, "Have you come here on your own?"

"No, I'm here with my three mates, they're at that coffee shop across the road."

Everybody looks out of a small, misty window to get a glimpse of them and we can see them standing on the other side of the road, staring blankly at the bar.

"Bring them in!" Dizza shouts.

I can't believe our luck. It feels so surreal to even be this close to them.

I text Len and tell them that the band wants them to come in. I look through the window again and I can see them all jumping around, hugging and fist-bumping each other. I shake my head, thinking they're going tarnish my hard grafting.

They walk into the bar a lot calmer than they were before, though, which makes me feel very relieved. I introduce everybody, and they get a drink at the bar and join us in the booth.

Time spirals as we spend hours drinking and laughing with the band and, eventually, they're saying that it's time they went back to the hotel. They must have seen our disappointment because Dizza jumps up from his seat and asks us to come with them to carry on the party.

We walk to the hotel together, each member of the group talking to a different member of the band. This time I'm with Dizza and I talk to him about our holiday, since I said this is our first time here, and he tells me stories about when he's been here. In no time, we're back at their hotel room and it's enormous, more like a suite, all decorated with clean white furniture and tasteful decorative pillows, with expensive artwork bringing life to the blank white walls. We sit on a group of sofas that surround a long glass coffee table. Dizza is flicking through some records in a cardboard box before putting one onto the turntable and placing the needle down gently. *Fools' Gold* by The Stone Roses begins to play, and I bop my head to the tune, singing along with Brown.

Beaker throws down a huge block of MD and coke onto the table. The four of us stare at the blocks, floating innocently on top of the glass. Jav looks at me with a concerned look on his face, waiting to see if any of us are going to go along with it. I shrug at him and whisper, "Fuck it." And he eventually follows course. The band start chopping up lines for everybody on the table.

"Dig in!" Freddy laughs and snorts a line that looked about fifty miles long, half the length of the table.

Dizza dances over and does the same, and so do

we, snorting our thin, powdery lines.

Half an hour goes by and we start to come up.

Dizza comes over to the table again. He's carrying a box and singing along to the song that's playing. I can't hear it very well over the high-pitched sirens deep within my ears, rattling my brain.

"Someone gave us this new board game... Dice Defenders," he reads off the box.

He pushes it along the table and we flick through the contents of the box. There are some character cards stacked up in a section of the box and so I decide to flick through them. They look amazing. All the colours on the card are jumping out and pulsating at me and everything about the character looks like its own thing; moles on their faces protrude in a way that screams for my focus, individual eyelashes stand to attention, sweeping in big exaggerated motions, sending a cold shiver down my spine. I flick to the next card. Wait... What? Is that me?

The card depicts a woman with long pink hair and piercings and her face looks the spitting image of mine. Her style is not at all like the rest of the characters, who are drawn in a quirky cartoon style and dressed in shiny knight's armour, or elegant capes if they're a wizard. In this card, she's wearing black trousers and a black shirt and the drawing is so utterly realistic it looks like a photograph. I read the stats on the card and they're all maximum level. I look at the top of the card to see the name. Felicity.

"Are you seeing this?" I slur in astonishment, showing everybody else the card. "That's me!"

Nobody else can believe their eyes, either.

Dizza picks the card out of my hand and inspects it closely and far away.

"Ha-haaaa, what the fuck, that's you!" He laughs and frisbees the card back down onto the table. It slowly spins around once it's landed on the table and us four watch it, hypnotized by the colour of her pink hair mixing with the sultry black. Soon, it begins to spin faster and faster, until the detailed drawing looks like nothing more than a circular blur.

I'm projected back to that night in the forest. I'm standing alone in the middle of Paradox Park and I can hear the screaming again, the screaming I knew I would never be able to forget. I don't want to, but I walk towards the noise again. As I get closer, I'm presented with the same scene as before, but it's Gaz, not Ollie, who is stood over someone, stabbing them and grunting with anger each time the knife ploughs into the body. But who is he stabbing? I don't know, I can't see.

I start to elevate into the air, getting a bird's eye view of the horror unfolding. Ryan is lying on the floor, looking up at me, staring into my eyes, and I'm staring back at his and they're filling with blood and his screaming becomes louder and higher and it rips me apart from the inside, again. My eyes blink rapidly as I come out of my trance. I lean back slowly and look at the other three sat near me. They're all coming out of it now, too. We look at each other, in silence. The noise of the band laughing and singing is the only soundtrack to this uncomfortable moment of waiting for somebody to say something.

"Did you see it again, too?" Jav whispers.

Nobody gives a verbal reply, we all just nod and blink stupidly.

The band come and sits back down on the sofas with us and it's obvious that they can tell something isn't right.

"What's up?" Beaker asks us all.

"You won't believe us if we tell you." Jav shakes his head slowly, looking at the floor.

"Try us!" Dizza offers.

I explain what happened that night, with Jenk and Len butting in sometimes to add in little details I missed out, and they sit there stunned with their mouths open.

"When you threw the card down, it sort of sent me back there. I saw it all again, but I saw Ryan and Gaz this time... maybe I'm remembering more," I explain, but not being certain at all.

"Did you see me stabbing him?" Len panics.

"Len, for God's sake, you didn't kill him!" Jenk spits.

"I know what I saw!" he shouts back.

"How can you see yourself stabbing someone?" Freddy asks, his eyes blazing.

"You can't," I answer for him.

"I don't know, but I did. I didn't mean to kill him," Len says.

"It definitely wasn't you, Len. I saw Gaz," Jav speaks up.

"So did I that time," Jenk admits.

"It must have been Gaz then, if we all saw him," I conclude.

"Sounds to me like drugs is your gateway to the truth," Dizza philosophises.

"It does! You've just got to do loads of drugs and then BOOM! Murder solved," Freddy laughs.

We look at each other and telepathically agree that that's what we have to do.

For our last night in Dam, we reckon we should go hard or go home, and since we're not ready to go home yet, that leaves us with only one option. So, we spend the entire day and night smoking as much as possible. We walk around the dark streets as if we're the only people in the world. Len is making fun of Jenk's name by shouting it in stupid voices, and for the tenth time in a minute, he shouts it again.

"Oh, Jenkies!"

I'm crying with laughter, as well as Jenkies himself.

"Len, shut up! People live here!" Jav demands.

"Oh Jenkies, Jav's angry!" he replies, even louder

than before.

We come across a fancy cheese shop on our travels and stop to have a look through the windows.

"They're obsessed with cheese here," I state.

"There's loads of cheese in there!" Len points out.

"Well, it is a cheese shop, Len," I reply.

"I'm taking a picture of this one, it looks well nice!" Jenk tells us, pulling his phone out of his pocket and snapping a picture of the triangle-shaped cheese with smooth concaves in it, coupled with an expensive bottle of wine, wrapped together in an elegant display case. A spotlight hangs above it to further impress anybody who has the pleasure of stumbling upon such a distinguished cheese.

We carry on walking once we've had our visual fill of cheese and we spot a nice bench atop a hill bending over a canal. Just as we're about to cross over the road, a giant, heavy-set black man stumbles towards us, slurring words we cannot understand. As he gets closer, and respectively scarier, the three lads decide they're going to run away up the hill across the road, but by the time I've realised the plan, a bicycle stops in front of me and the man, leaving me trapped with him on the opposite side of the road. The man on the bike starts to talk to him and so I take the opportunity to sneak away and rush up the hill, finally catching up with the group.

"That was well scary!" Len shouts to me, smiling

and laughing.

"Yeah, and you all just fucking left me with him," I begin, but I'm in too good a mood to be angry, so I leave that rant, for now.

We sit down on the bench and talk about whatever's on our minds, apparently.

"Dunno if you've ever done it, but I shaved my armpits for the first time and honestly it feels amazing," Jav brings up out of the blue.

"Yeah! Flic told me to do it and I actually prefer it now, I'm so smooth," Len joins in.

"Well, I shaved my armpits before either of you two did, so I'm a trendsetter," I say in a sassy tone, but not seriously.

"It'd be a bit minging if you didn't," Jav responds.

"Yeah!" Len and Jenk agree respectively.

"That's so horrible! I might just stop shaving now."

"I wouldn't be your friend," Jav jokes (hopefully).

"Would you be my friend if I looked like this?" I ask and then tuck my top lip underneath itself so that my teeth hang out over the rest of my mouth.

"Nah, I wouldn't even speak to you," Len answers.

"Maybe, but I'd have to punch you in the face every now and again," Jenk adds.

"Alright, fuckin' 'ell, thought we were having a laugh here!" I say, trying not to find it funny, but I can't help but laugh.

The sun begins to rise as we sit on the cold bench – it's been a 24-hour sesh and we're definitely feeling it now.

As a direct result of having had no sleep at all, everybody is silent the entire car ride to the airport. When we arrive, we settle down on a group of chairs to have a rest. Jav falls asleep across the back wall, spread out across at least five chairs, whereas Jenk is asleep sat upright with his mouth hanging open. I rest my head on Len's knee but the immense ganjover is making it impossible to fall asleep. We all agree we've never felt so stale.

Once we're back at Manchester airport, we sit waiting for Jav's dad to pick us up, but we can't get a word out of Javan at all. I don't think I've ever seen anyone look more depressed. It's almost becoming his default pose now, to have his chin resting on his palm and his lips hanging down into a puffy, sulky pout.

His dad picks us up and we get dropped off at home, going our separate ways.

With everyone else dropped home, Jav and his dad drive back to their house. Jav is somehow even quieter than before. He has his earphones in and is looking out the window, almost facing away from his dad in the driver's seat.

"Did you enjoy it then?" his dad asks him,

glancing at him for a slight second before looking back at the road in front.

"Alright," Jav replies quietly and shrugs, his face still sulking.

His dad continues to try and make conversation, but Jav offers no more than one-word answers to everything.

"What did you get up to while you were there?" he asks.

"Stuff," Jav replies.

They pull up into the driveway and Jav gets out of the car swiftly without saying a word. His mum can barely swing the door open before he heads straight through and goes up the stairs, into his room and locks the door. He lies down on top of the bed and stares at the ceiling. His mum comes up the stairs and knocks on his bedroom door.

"Are you alright, Jav?" she asks him concernedly.

"Tired!" he shouts back through the door.

She asks him if he wants any dinner, but he says no, and with that she sighs and leaves him alone, heading back downstairs to finish her TV programme.

What's going through his mind is unfathomable for anybody outside of it. What makes matters worse is he doesn't even know what's going on himself. Everybody knows when there's something wrong with someone, but what is there to do when nobody can explain what it is? Javan's world was by no means inadequate; his family was always there for him, he always had a good group of friends around him, but for some, that just isn't enough.

He lies on his bed for around two hours, staring into space, thinking about nothing, before he finally plucks up the courage within himself. He takes a belt from his bedside cabinet and ties it around the coat hook at the top of his wardrobe. He pulls the belt over his head and lines it up comfortably around his long, slender neck. He takes a deep breath and scans his bedroom with his eyes. Will he miss it? Or will he be missed in it? The only answer he can conjure is 'no.' So he slides off the base of the wardrobe, his heart full of the pain of isolation, his eyes full of sorrowful tears. The belt cracks as it stretches under his weight, the pull springing him back up momentarily. As he takes his final breaths, his eyes dart around his skull, looking everywhere they can before they fill with darkness because suddenly, a wave of regret washes over his twitching being. *I will miss it. I will be missed.* But of course, it is all too late for Javan. His body swings from side to side, making an ominous thudding noise each time it hits against his brown wooden wardrobe. His parents wonder what this noise is from the living room downstairs, but decide to ignore it. He won't be discovered hanging there until the following evening.

NINE DAYS LATER:
A WELCOME HOME SURPRISE

A fter sleeping all day to recover from Dam, I suddenly feel the urge to get back into it and go out with them all to smoke again, so I message the group chat.

Anyone fancy going out?

Jenk and Len reply instantly saying 'yes', but Jav doesn't even read the message. We say we'll wait an hour for him to reply and if he doesn't, we'll just go out without him.

I decide to text Len whilst we wait to see if he replies.

Do you reckon there's something going on with Jav? He's been acting weird since Dam.

Who knows, he can be like that sometimes.

You should have seen his face when we walked

back to meet them that night we got together, he looked so upset.

Maybe he fancies you, Flic ;)

But that isn't the first time somebody's said that, maybe he's right.

Jav still hasn't read the message yet so I start getting ready to go out.

I walk into the front room and my dad is the only one in there.

"Come here, I'll show you a card trick," he says, smiling to himself and sitting cross-legged on the floor.

I sit down in front of him and watch him set out the cards.

"Right. You shuffle those, I'll shuffle these," he says and we both mirror each other as we laugh and shuffle the cards, looking more like each other than we ever have before.

"Okay, so this side is red, and this side is black. Deal the cards and put them in whichever colour you think they are," he instructs.

I deal the cards out, using instinct to put them into the right lines. He starts laughing as I have to shuffle backwards to fit all the cards in the line.

"Look," he says, once I've put all the cards down.

He flips the cards over and they're in piles of red and black. I look up from the cards to look at him and he does the same, both of us smiling at each other.

145

"I am so good. Am I magic, or are you?" I laugh, and he does, too. "How do you do it?" I ask excitedly.

He explains how it works to me and I slightly understand it. He sits back down in his regular spot and I get a drink out of the fridge to take out with me. I tell him I'm going out as I'm exiting the room.

"Okay, hun. Love you, be safe," he shouts through the doors. "Are you feeling well enough to go out?"

"Of course. Love you too." I say it back.

———

For a change of scenery, we smoke on the football fields instead of Paradox. At ten o'clock, the summer nights start to get darker but are still just as warm. We talk about our holiday again now that we're all more energetic. We rave for hours about meeting Tenacious Toes. Laughing about Jav in the taxi home after the England game throws Len into a fit of coughing, which always sounds like he's throwing up as his big, juicy lips vibrate off each other.

"You need to get a new cough, this one makes me feel sick every time," I tell him.

"Just stop trying to muffle it, Len!" Jenk joins in, feeling the same way as I do.

Len takes a moment to himself to stop coughing so much.

"How's this then? Cough number one, *cough*!" He trials his first cough.

"Not the best..." I give him my honest opinion.

"Still sounds like you're throwing up," Jenk adds again.

"Cough number two, *cough*!"

"There we go! I like cough number two."

"Yeah, it's a proper cough, that one," Jenk and I praise him.

Len's customisation session is interrupted by his phone ringing obnoxiously loudly. It's his dad.

"I'm well too high to answer this now," he declares and pushes his phone back into his pocket.

It rings a few more times and he continues to ignore it, texting him instead to see what he wants.

You need to come home now, Len.

I'm out with Flic and Jenk though.

Bring them too, you all need to hear this.

Len reads the texts aloud and we all look at each other worriedly.

"What the hell's going on?" I ask, even though I know they don't know, either.

We clamber into the car and drive over to Len's house. His dad greets us at the door looking solemn, and ushers us into the living room where we are joined by Len's mum who looks equally grave. We're definitely in trouble, but they don't look angry.

"Come and sit down, you three," says Len's dad, motioning us to a three-seater sofa.

We do as we are told.

"We're guessing you haven't heard the news

147

then?" Len's dad asks us, the three clueless, paranoid teenagers huddled on the sofa with confused expressions on our faces.

"What news?" Len answers for us all.

"Javan's dad has just rung me. I'm really sorry to have to tell you that they found Javan dead in his room," he explains, trying to be strong for us but showing just the right amount of sympathy. "Poor boy."

"*What?*" Len shouts out of shock.

Jenk blows a big gust of air out of his mouth. His heart sinks as he stands up with his hand on his forehead and leaves the room the way we came in.

I can't believe it. I'm devastated because one of my best friends of fourteen years is gone. I'm angry at him because he didn't speak to me when he needed to. I'm also strangely relieved for him, because I know he's in a better place and perhaps he has found some happiness and peace there which eluded him in life.

"I can't believe it." I shake my head. Other than that, I'm speechless.

"I know, it is so unexpected," Len's dad says, joining me with a headshake.

"I wonder why he did it?" Len's mum ponders to herself.

Jenk returns to the room with a lost look on his face and we all stay there together for a while, not saying anything and just staring into space.

I check the time and see that it's one in the morning.

"We should go home. A bit of sleep will probably help us all," I say, standing up from the couch.

"Do you want a lift home?" Len's dad asks me and Jenk.

"I should be alright. Thanks, though." I manage to crack a forced smile.

I say goodnight to his parents and Len walks Jenk and I to the front door. As Jenk is putting his shoes on, I stand in front of Len and look into his eyes, neither of us saying a word. I lunge forward and give him a big, tight hug, I don't know whether it is to make him feel better, or myself, but it helps nonetheless. Jenk and Len have a quick hug, too and Jenk walks out the door towards my car. Len leans down and kisses me on both cheeks, my forehead and then my lips, each feeling so soft and gentle on my face.

"I love you," he whispers.

"I love you, too," I whisper back, and smile.

The journey around the corner to Jenk's house is quiet. We just mutter passing comments to each other, never forming a proper conversation. We get to the house and I give him a hug before telling him to take care.

Nobody is awake when I get home, so I crawl into bed and video call with Len. We speak a little bit about Jav, and seeing his face on the tiny phone screen makes me feel a hundred times more comforted.

Soon enough, I fall asleep, dreaming about the four of us together for one last time.

TEN DAYS LATER: (THE NEXT DAY)
AN ANTICIPATED VISIT

I wake up in the afternoon with a text from Len:
The police have been round to talk about Jav and that night at Paradox. My mum and dad are fuming. They'll probably be coming to yours soon, so watch out.

My heart skips a beat as I read it, and I can't even reply before I'm out of bed and throwing up in the bathroom. My mum comes up the stairs to check on me.

"Are you alright, darling?" she asks, as she peers around the door to look at me seated on the edge on the bath.

"No," I reply bluntly, wiping the tears from my eyes.

"What's the matter?" She sits down next to me.

"Jav killed himself, we found out last night. I

think the police are coming around to talk to me," I explain to her.

She expresses her shock and gives me a hug, keeping her arm around me as we talk some more.

The doorbell rings, and my dad answers. We stay quiet in the bathroom, trying to hear the conversation downstairs. He shouts my name and tells me to come down.

"Hello, Felicity?" A small policeman with big ears and a little pea head asks me to identify myself. He is standing just outside the front door, having not yet been permitted entry by my dad.

"Yeah, that's me."

"We'd like to talk to you about your friend Javan, if that's okay?" he says, motioning to the other policeman stood next to him, this one being much taller and bigger in every way.

"Yeah, no problem," I say and open the door wider to let them step inside the house.

We sit in the study, both policemen facing me, leaving me feeling more like a criminal than a mere witness.

"First of all, we're sorry about what happened to your friend, Javan. We understand that this is going to be a hard time for you, so we won't push you too hard with our questioning. To begin with, do you have any idea why Javan may have committed suicide?" the small officer begins.

"He's been badly depressed for a couple of years

now, he was self-harming and stuff already," I explain, as I rub my hands together nervously.

"Do you think it could have had anything to do with the night you were in Paradox Park? The night of the murder," the larger officer asks me, looking straight into my eyes. The icy blueness of them sends a familiar shiver down my spine.

"I have no idea. It did shake us all up, though, so I couldn't say for sure if it was or wasn't a factor... Can I ask if you've got any information on the murder?" I hesitate to ask.

"We can't give you any information on the case at this moment in time," the bigger officer says sternly.

I nod and look down at my hands and realise my leg is shaking.

"Can you tell us what happened that night, please, Felicity?"

I take a deep breath and I physically feel the colour drain from the top of my head right down to my toes. I apologise and run upstairs to the bathroom to throw up.

My mum walks into the study whilst I'm gone and explains my illness to them. They seem to be understanding; the bigger officer less so, however.

I come back in after five minutes and apologise again. Mum asks if I need anything else as she passes me a glass of water, and I say no.

"Well... We went to Paradox at about eleven o'clock. We sat on the bench at the back of the field, near the tree. We were there for around two hours when someone approached the bench. He sat with us and he said his name was Gaz and told us he was hiding from the police because he'd just beaten up his brother. Then he disappeared into the bushes behind us. We decided to stay there and just forget about him, but then, a while later –"

"How long is a while later?" the big officer interrupts me.

"Probably about half an hour, maybe more. Erm... so, then we got up because we could hear screaming, we walked towards it and I saw..." I stop myself. I don't actually know what I saw, and I can't tell these two why.

"What did you see, Felicity?" the small officer asks.

"I think I saw Gaz, stabbing a boy from the year below me at school. His mum came looking for him that night, but we hadn't seen him. She was pretty frantic, so I assume he's been missing for a while."

"You *THINK?* In your written statement you say something about a bana –" the big officer says but is then spoken over by the other officer, who I prefer to listen to.

"We have a case of a missing teenager named Ryan in that area. Is that the boy you're talking about?" he asks.

"Yes, that's him!"

He nods and writes something down, but he

doesn't confirm whether it was Ryan that was murdered, and says that he isn't allowed to tell me any details yet. But I try and get a quick peek at one of their notebooks, only seeing what I think is the word 'weapon', until the big officer snaps the book to his chest, glaring at me. They thank me for my time after a few more questions and they leave. Then I have to revisit the whole ordeal to explain to my parents why the police needed to talk to me.

TWO WEEKS LATER:

NAH, I'M GAY, HUN

It's Javan's funeral today. It's being held at Poston Gardens, a beautiful place with a grand country hall in the centre, surrounded by elegant flower gardens, vast amounts of greenery, a zoo, a chapel and a crematorium. Len, Jenk and I all arrive together. Our parents also attend for a short while, just to pay their respects and give their condolences to Jav's family. The service for Jav is how I expect it to be. His parents and sisters all read out a passage or letter for him through their sorrowful tears, not forgetting to mention the fact that he was extremely depressed, and nobody knew why, which is true, but there must be something more, something he hasn't told anybody.

His parents had asked us three if we wanted to say anything, but we'd declined. I don't know about the other two, but I somehow didn't feel qualified enough because I felt like, despite knowing him my whole life, I never really knew the real Javan at all. Not since high school, anyway. So what was I supposed to say? "He was a great guy, at least from what I knew of him"? But anyway, the service is nice. They play some Tenacious Toes, which was our idea; we considered it our contribution rather than speeches.

After all of the tributes, we take a stroll through Poston Gardens towards the pub where a gathering was being held, Jav's family leading the crowd. My phone vibrates in my pocket and I pull it out, dropping to the back of the parade to read the message. It's from Laurie:

Are you still at Pozzy Gs?

Yeah, why?

I'll be there soon. How are you?

Yeah, I'm alright. I'll tell you about the service when I see you. In a bit!

Jenk and Len fall back too and Jenk whispers to me, "Want to do this LSD now?" he grins. "For Jav."

I look around and nobody seems to have noticed we're gone, so I agree.

We trudge deeper into the wooded area next to the path we're walking on and find a circle of tree stumps to sit on.

Jenk pulls out a sheet of blotters, painted with

colourful cartoons of elephants which vividly remind me of the ones I saw in Paradox.

"To Jav," I say and hold my tiny square up in the air, laughing at how absurd it is to make a toast to the dead with a little slice of acid.

But Len and Jenk hold theirs up, too and repeat, "To Jav."

We place the squares under our tongues and wait.

"What did you think of the service then?" I ask them both.

"Was alright, wasn't it?" Jenk nods.

"Bit weird how they really hammered on about the fact that he was depressed. It was almost as if it was forced," I ponder, with them both agreeing immediately.

"Did you see anyone else from school?" Len asks.

"Nah, did you?" Jenk replies, to which Len shakes his head 'no.'

After only around fifteen minutes, I already start to feel something. I get goosebumps all over my arms and my limbs feel numb and weak. But it doesn't panic me, I just sit there and think about Javan's funeral whilst we wait a little bit longer for the trip to intensify.

Twenty minutes later, I open my eyes, from having them closed for a minute, and look at Len. His body is rippling from the top to the bottom and so is Jenks'.

I look at my phone to read the message from Laurie and the letters swirl around the screen in all different directions, making it impossible to read. Everything I see is pulsing in the shape of a star, but I manage to send a quick reply:

In the forest.

I begin to laugh uncontrollably, and my legs can't stop shaking. Len is talking about something and he looks really excited about it, but I can't hear the words he's saying, it just sounds like a muffled droning noise. The more I listen to it, the deeper into the trip I get. The sun is shining through the trees and is hitting me right in the face.

"I'm going to lie down here," I say, as I get up from the log and lie down, using my jacket as a pillow to prop up against a tree.

As I lie there, feeling very stable, I can enjoy the trip more. I look up at them both sitting above me, and my eyes slam shut all of a sudden and everything goes black. When I open them again, Gaz's face is centimeters away from mine and he's smiling, displaying his crooked teeth and I can hear those screams again. He slashes the knife at my body, but I feel no pain. Everything goes black and silent once again, and when I open my eyes this time, I see Phillip from work and he does the same, showing off his artificially white smile as he stabs my body with a knife, the screaming getting louder and louder. It goes black once more and when I open my eyes this time, Len is there, leaning over me.

"Are you okay?" he drones, with an equally expressionless face.

"Yeah, I'm okay," I reply sceptically.

"Good," he says.

Then he smiles his wide grin, that I've seen and fallen in love with many times before, but then he stabs me in the chest. As the screams travel closer to me, I realise something... it's not Ryan, it's a girl. I look up at my killer one last time, and I can't believe my eyes. My killer is me.

I come out of my trance with a big exhalation of air, and Laurie is leaning over me.

"Are you okay?" she asks worriedly.

"...Yeah..." I reply, waiting for the moment when I get stabbed again.

"Good. Thought you were dying," she quips and gives me a hand up.

I'm still tripping but I'm much more sober than I was before so it's easier for me to answer all the questions I get from Laurie.

"What happened?" she asks, sitting down next to me on another log.

"I closed my eyes for a second and when I opened them again, Gaz was so close to my face and he smiled and he stabbed me and then I closed them again and then when I opened them this time it was Phillip and he stabbed me and then I closed them again and then when I opened them the next time, I saw..." I pause, remembering about how scared Len was when he thought he was the one who had murdered Ryan.

"Saw what?" Len asks, staring right at me with his innocent eyes and his beautiful face.

"Erm... I got stabbed again. And then I woke up." I quickly conjure up the rest of the hallucination.

"That's mad. Bet it was well scary," Len comments, staring off into the distance as if he was planning on hallucinating the same thing himself.

As a way of being able to talk to Laurie alone, I say I need the toilet and she volunteers to go with me without me having to hint to her in any way.

Of course, we have a spliff on the walk there, since that's the only reason she met up with us. We get to the flower gardens and I tell her that I don't need the toilet, I just need to talk to her and so we sit down on a wooden memorial bench.

"I'm getting so confused with all these different things I'm seeing, Laurie. I don't know what's real and what isn't," I explain to her. "I saw Len stabbing me, but I didn't want to worry him again, and just before I woke up, I saw myself."

"There's no way it was Len, or you," she confirms.

"I know, but there must be a reason why I saw it."

"Maybe it's just because he's been thinking it's him as well. Your mind is just playing tricks on you."

"I hope so." I drop my head.

Laurie is about to say something in reply, but she's stopped in her tracks by a bride and groom walking slowly across the field and stopping in front of us. They're followed shortly by a photographer, who prompts them on how to pose. We look at each other, wondering if they're going to ask us to move, but they don't. Laurie and I appear in the background of every photo they take, sitting on a bench, tripping out my arse.

Finally, they leave and go to take pictures elsewhere, probably somewhere that has a better view than two druggies on a bench. We get up and walk in the opposite direction. Two priests approach us on the pathway and ask us if we'd like to enter the church to find Christ or repent our sins.

"Nah, I'm Jewish," I shrug.

"Nah, I'm gay, hun," Laurie replies at the same time.

They frown and shake their heads before walking away from us.

Now is not the time for confessions.

We go back to meet the lads and they've come out of the forest to kick the ball around. Me and Laurie join in, but my senses are not prepared for this amount of coordination and I keep missing the ball, or just kicking it in the opposite direction to anybody. They keep telling me how easy football is and that I should be able to do it. Something changes inside of me and I can feel it in my brain. Suddenly, I'm like the best footballer in the world. I scoop up the ball with my foot and flick it up into the air before kicking it up a few more times and volleying it over to Len.

"Do it again," Len says, thinking it's a fluke.

The ball comes towards me and I look at Laurie, indicating that I'm going to pass it to her. I flick the ball up and kick it over to her and we keep the ball in the air for about a minute before I use the inside of my foot to hit it over to Jenkies.

"I am football!" I say in all seriousness but joking on the inside.

Jenk throws the ball back to me and I chip it up into the air again. I kick it even higher so that I have time to spin around and I bicycle-kick the ball straight into Len's hands. I roll over onto my front to see their faces and they all look amazed.

"Why am I suddenly good at it?" I laugh and stand up, taking a seat for a moment to have a drink and watch them play.

I join back into the game. Laurie kicks the ball to me, and I attempt to flick the ball up again, but it slides off the side of my foot this time.

"Wait, what?" I gawp.

I get the ball back and try it again and this time it

doesn't even get over the toe of my shoe and I just kick it over to Jenkies.

"I've lost it! Why did I have a break?"

Everyone laughs again as I've been knocked back into reality, continuing to play badly for the rest of the game. But at least for five minutes, I WAS FOOTBALL!

A group of us choose to go out into town to have a few drinks in Jav's honour. Laurie, Jenkies, Len, Jav's sisters and I all head out in a minibus. The pub is already packed by the time we get there so we go straight into a small nightclub tucked away on the corner of the street. Jav's sisters go inside ahead of us whilst we have a fag outside the gates.

"How are you lot feeling now?" Laurie asks us.

"Mmm, it's a sad day," Len replies.

I nod in agreement.

"I couldn't stop looking at the priest's hair, though," Jenk admits.

"He did look like an iced gem, to be fair," I suggest.

I look around to see who's out tonight, and I don't instantly see anybody I recognise.

Somebody walks up next to me and grabs my arm.

"Alright, Flic?" a male voice says.

I turn around and see Scary Lee towering over me with a smile.

"Oh. Alright, Lee?" I smile back, stepping away slightly so I don't have to strain my neck as much.

"You look fit as always," he says in his chavvy voice, followed by a cheeky laugh.

I let out a feeble laugh that almost mimics his and say, "Thanks".

"Mind not saying that about my girlfriend when I'm stood right here, mate?" Len intervenes.

"What's ye fuckin' problem, mate?" Lee starts squaring up.

"You!" Len leans into him abruptly.

Scary Lee looks like he's going to batter Len, but he looks down at me, takes a deep breath and steps away, then starts to walk off down the road.

"Scary Lee? More like Dairy Lee!" Len shouts after him.

He turns back around and within only a few strides, he is face-to-face with Len again, and he punches him square in the nose, knocking him over onto the pavement. Onlookers start to surround the commotion and Scary Lee notices. He begins to hurry off, but turns around to me and says sorry before he darts away.

I turn to look at Len, who's sitting on the kerb holding his nose.

"You deserved that one, you idiot!" I laugh, knowing he isn't in as much pain as he thinks he is.

"Oh my God, I think my nose is falling off! Jenk, is my nose falling off? Flic, what if my nose falls off?" he panics.

I kneel down in front of him. "Move your hands, let's see the damage," I tell him, moving his hands out of the way myself.

I scan his face, not seeing a single bruise or drop of blood anywhere.

"Think you're fine, mate," I say, slapping him on the arm and standing up.

The surrounding crowd then loses interest and split off as well, once they see there's no injuries.

"Shall we go in?" I ask the group and they all say yes, apart from Len who's now feeling a bit sorry for himself.

Laurie asks if I want to come to the toilet for a bit of ching, so naturally I agree. We squeeze into the tiny cubicle and she pulls out the little bag, full to the brim of white powder. I have to use the nail of my little finger to scoop up the powder since Laurie has no nails of her own. I put my finger under her nostril, and she sniffs in the bugger sugar. I collect a bump for myself and we head out of the bathroom. We're spotted by a couple of Laurie's colleagues, Gina and Kat, and they grab our hands and pull us onto the dance floor.

It's only about ten minutes until Laurie's asking me to go to the bathroom again, but how could I say no? We get into the cubicle again and Laurie digs into her pocket to find the bag.

"Have you got it?" she asks.

"No, I gave it back to you," I reply.

"Well, I've not got it," she panics.

We stand there for a minute whilst she checks every single pocket, but to no avail.

"Ohhh shit, there was so much sniff in there," she cries.

"Well, it's only going to be on the dance floor so let's just retrace our steps," I plan.

We hurry out of the bathroom, scouring the floor for the tiny bag. I see Laurie bending down and picking something up and she just looks at me and heads back to the bathroom. We push into the same cubicle as before and she holds up the bag, voicing her relief through a big sigh. We have an extra big bump for our troubles.

Later on in the night, Laurie and I sit in the smoking area outside. We've had a few drinks and a good dance by now. We sit on a round wooden bench and light a cig. A middle-aged man stumbles out of a set of wooden double doors with a cigarette limply placed between his fingers, snaking from a bony, limp wrist. He has a pair of rectangle glasses, a bald head, buttoned white shirt and a lovely pair of saggy, white cargo shorts. He zigzags towards the bench and asks if anyone has a lighter, which I do. I hold the lighter up towards him and he leans forward, hovering his cigarette above the flame. I lift the lighter higher to light it, but he moves higher too. This happens again three times before I lose my patience.

"What are you doing? Do you want me to light it or not?" I snap.

"I'm just using the air of the flame," he slurs.

"The *what*?" I ask, in a very exaggerated tone.

"It makes it taste more organic, no?" He waves his hand elegantly through the air.

"Nah," I laugh and shake my head. "Just use the flame," I order and hold the lighter up to his face again.

"Oh, right. Cheers." He shrugs off his beliefs about using the air of the flame and lights his cig before wandering off and standing with a group of people.

Laurie's work friends appear from behind us and they look at the man who left us merely seconds ago.

"Who's Mr Cargo Shorts over there?" Gina nods towards him.

"Dunno, I think it's someone's dad. Absolute weirdo," I say, making a long story short.

"Just thought I'd warn you, Georgie-Anne's here." Gina raises one side of her mouth in concern.

"Where?" Laurie asks, looking worried.

"She was inside last time I saw her," she replies, starting to look around to make sure she's not wrong.

"Nah, there she is, our Grievous," I whisper, pointing to Georgie-Anne just as she walks out of the doorway on the other side of the court.

We call her Grievous because not only are her initials GBH, but she's also been nicked for that a few times. She's a big girl, one that you wouldn't want to mess with. Her face always rests in the same grimacing position, as if she is constantly smelling something disgusting, which she probably is, since she smells like distant cheese. And her head is merely a blob that sits atop another blob (her body). She is wearing a blue denim shirt that is ten sizes too small, exposing her muffin top, and a pair of blue denim jeans, equally undersized.

"What the fuck is she wearing?" Laurie laughs, knowing that it will trigger a long chain of insults.

"She looks cool, mate. Georgie-Anne Van Damme," I join in.

"How has she not had the death penalty yet?"

"They tried to stone her once, but it didn't work, she enjoyed it and now she does it five times a day."

We can't help but burst out laughing at her, as we've done many times before. Unfortunately, this time, she notices.

She comes storming over to us and I find my eyes quickly scanning her hands, just to make sure there's not a knife clasped in her clammy grip.

"What the fuck are yeh doin'?" she screams, as

her mouth widens to reveal a small slither of orange skin covering one of her teeth.

Her shouting and furious run over to us has attracted an audience around us now, and everybody notices the mess that's in her mouth, whispering about it to each other and laughing.

We fall silent for a moment, not really knowing what to say, and the tension runs high as everybody around waits for someone to speak.

"You've got a bit of baked bean skin on your teeth, babes," Laurie replies, throwing everyone into a fit of drunken, over-the-top laughter, like a group of pissed hyenas in a comedy club.

In an embarrassed rage, she licks the bean from her tooth, picks up a beer bottle from the bench and twats it against the side of Laurie's head. Laurie falls off the bench and onto the floor, clutching her head as thick red blood trickles through her fingers. Laurie's colleague, Kat, comes bounding over and roundhouse-kicks Georgia-Anne in the head before tackling her to the ground and attempting to control her, as she thrashes around, trying to get another shot at Laurie.

"Who's that?" I hear someone shout in amazement.

"That's Kat Koolburn," Gina informs them as she rushes over to Laurie.

I kneel down next to my sister with tears

streaming out of my eyes, struggling to say anything that isn't a swear word.

"Oh fuck. Oh shit. Are you okay? *Ohhhhh* shit, shit, shit!" I panic, putting my hand over hers on her head, as if that is going to help in some way.

She doesn't reply. She can't reply.

Thankfully, someone calls an ambulance, and it arrives in under a minute. I get in the ambulance with her and ring Len to tell him I've left and that I love him. Police are also on the scene quickly and Georgie-Anne is swiftly arrested. I'll be petitioning for the death penalty.

I'm standing in the patio area at the side of my grandma's house, staring down at a large greyhound dog that's barking excitedly at me. I put my hands out, attempting to calm it down, but that only seems to make it more excited. Suddenly, it takes two big lunges towards me and, for some reason, I run towards it as well. Big mistake. The dog flips over onto its back and kangaroo-kicks me in the stomach. I double over and hold onto my stomach as the pain courses through my body. I run to the kitchen door and close it just enough so that the dog can't get its head through. I start taunting it by thrusting my middle finger into its face outside of the crack in the door and pulling my hand back inside the door when it jumps to bite my finger off. I do this for what feels like ten minutes before standing up and walking into the front room.

Next thing I know, I'm on a train to Manchester. I have my earphones in and I'm innocently typing on my laptop on the tray in front of me. With me I have a small suitcase, my backpack and a coat and a jacket are slung over the arm of the chair next to me. I look into the aisle of the train and see that a row of people has just walked on. I look out the window to see where we are. Manchester. My stop, exactly.

The words, "Next stop, Nottingham," ring through the speakers on the train. I close the laptop and hurriedly try to pick everything up at the same time. I rush down the aisle and finally make it to the doors, but they close in front of me and the train starts to pull away from the platform. I look through the window leading into the train driver's cockpit and a bald man with glasses shakes his head and shrugs.

"You're out of time," echoes loudly through my head.

I'm woken by my arms flying out above me and falling back down onto my head. I roll over and force myself back to sleep.

"Next stop, Nottingham" rings through the speakers again as I rush to collect my possessions. I run down the aisle and see the doors closing. I just manage to squeeze through before the doors shut and

I set everything down on the wooden bench on the platform.

"Aah, just in time," echoes softly through my brain.

I attempt to open my eyes but a bright, artificial light forces them shut again. I take my time, opening one eye slightly first, and then the other. I'm lying across a row of green plastic chairs that I must have lined up last night. To my right, Laurie lies sleeping in a hospital bed, her head wrapped in a white bandage. I rub my face as I attempt to find my glasses. The inside of my nose is completely numb from all the ching and my stomach is flipping from my hangover, but I push it all to the back of my mind because I can't even imagine how Laurie is feeling this morning.

A young female nurse walks up and picks up the clipboard on the end of the hospital bed.

"Looks like you had a good night." She raises an eyebrow at me as she skims the paper.

She wakes Laurie up and asks her how she's feeling. My sister's voice is croaky and her eyes are barely open. She hovers her hand over the bandage in pain and groans, but she's okay. I sit with her for a few hours more before going home after Mum and Dad arrive.

THREE WEEKS LATER:
THE BIG REVEAL

Laurie is chilling in the front room, a bandage still on her head.

I walk in, and we sit watching the news on TV.

"I still haven't seen anything about this murder in Paradox. Have you?" she says to me.

"Nah, I've not... I'm starting to think it just wasn't even real."

"What do you mean?" she asks.

"Well, obviously something happened, the police came round. But..."

"What?" she insists.

"I don't know. We know nothing about what happened, we all saw something

different and we were proper monged that night. I just think we're creating it all in our minds. Putting links where there aren't any," I explain.

"Mmm, I see what you mean. Has anyone seen Ryan?"

"I wouldn't know. None of us have seen him, though and when the police came round they said that he's missing. But his mum hasn't been back and I haven't heard anything about him since."

"I would just forget about it then, he's probably back home now," she reassures me.

Suddenly, a new story pops up on the screen and the newsreader's voice drones:

"Police have been investigating the murder of an as yet unidentified young man in a local forest. The body had been extremely mutilated and forensic investigators discovered no DNA of the killer on the body and nobody has come forward with any leads on the victim or the killer. A sketch artist has created two images of what we believe the victim looked like before the vicious attack. We're looking for any possible witnesses who were in the area to come forward. If you have any information, please contact the number or e-mail onscreen, now."

I don't recognise either of the drawings of the victim at all, but something looks familiar. What is it? Laurie looks at me, concerned, noticing my immense concentration.

"Yeah, that's not Ryan... Do you want to go for a spliff?" I ask, knowing what her response will be, meaning I won't have to share my thoughts and feelings about the sketches.

"Defo," she replies.

We get in the car and drive around the corner to skin up and smoke our spliff.

On the way home, just as we roll down the long, narrow drive, our neighbour appears, looking like she's eager for a chat.

"Shit, Laurie, go-go-go-go!" I order her to zoom into the drive so we can get away.

"I can't!" she panics.

Our neighbour's face transitions from a chirpy smile to a puzzled frown as she watches us crawl past her in the car, both of us looking quizzical, me reading a page of the newspaper that I picked up from the footwell of the passenger side in a bid to look distracted.

We park up in the drive and run to the door, Laurie fumbling for her keys, desperately trying to put the key into the lock.

"Hiya!" she shouts over to us, just as we get the door open and run inside.

"That was a close one." I raise my eyebrows at Laurie.

"Well close," she reiterates.

A few hours later, I get a text from Javan's mum asking if I'd go round to help sort through Javan's stuff. She knows I knew him the best out of everyone. I agree and set off straight away.

She takes me straight upstairs to his room and she lets me look around for a moment silently.

"I've just started on that drawer next to his bed if you want to do that?" she begins.

"Oh. Yeah, I'll do that." I nod and sit on the edge of his bed, picking out a few stacks of paper.

"Can I get you a drink or anything, Flic?" she asks.

"I'll just have a water, please," I say, with a smile.

She walks out of the room and heads to the kitchen.

I open the first piece of paper on the top of the pile. It's a hand-written note, and I know straight away that it's Jav's handwriting.

July 5th, 2018

I've been keeping this secret for too long; I can't take it anymore. How can I keep such strong feelings to myself? Well, I can't! I've had to watch them both grow closer to each other right in front of my eyes. And that night in Amsterdam was too much for me to handle. I've felt this way for years but have never done anything about it. Well, I'm ready to do something now. Something big. Something he can't ignore. Something much more committed than just slashing my wrists for him. I love you, Len.

I sit looking at the note for what feels like forever, with my mouth hanging open. He killed himself for Len? This is getting more and more fucked-up every day.

Jav's mum shuffles back into the room and I fold the note back in half and put it at the bottom of the pile. I take the glass and say "Thank you", placing it on the side and continuing to sift through the notes.

July 3rd, 2018

They're officially together now but I've suspected it for a while, they've both been acting significantly happier than usual. We took shrooms again today, thankfully went better than last time. I think I'll do them again tomorrow. I just can't seem to enjoy myself on this holiday. She's sharing a room with him, not me! She should be sharing with Jenk instead. But there's nothing I can do but try and enjoy myself. I saw them tonight hugging and kissing and crying, I think they said they were in love. She will never love him as much as I do! She doesn't hurt herself for him like I do! He is mine.

What is going on!? I can't help but rush to read the next note, which, according to the date, is the night of the murder.

June 27th, 2018

I tried shrooms for the first time tonight. I don't know if I rate them, to be honest. I didn't really get much time alone with Len tonight, either. And this guy called Gaz turned up, everyone thought we were going to die, I wasn't too worried, he would have been doing me a favour. If anything, the bad trip made me really want him to kill me, but he didn't, obviously. I started tripping really badly after that. I saw myself on the battlefield and a German was shouting at me to fight and I couldn't, I never could. Maybe it's telling me what I should do.

I think we saw a murder, too, and Len seems to think it was him. He can't go to jail, he can't leave me! I carved his name into my thigh last night and it's starting to sting, I think it might be infected. But that just shows how devoted I am to him.

I close my eyes and feel pain in my heart for Javan. Nobody knew this secret life he was living.

I finally decide what to do with my findings.

"I know why he killed himself now," I say to his mum.

She looks at me and frowns, so I pass her the notes and watch her face as she reads them.

It takes around ten minutes for her to read as much as she can take.

"You did drugs together?" She looks me in the eyes.

"We didn't force him to do anything he didn't want to," I explain.

"Doesn't sound like it. He's miserable in these letters!"

"He was always miserable, he was depressed," I say, staying calm, trying not to raise my voice as she did.

She can't think of what to say. She stays curled up on her knees on the floor looking down at the letters resting on her lap.

"I had no idea. You know I would have tried to help, or at least let you know about it, if I had. I showed you the letters, didn't I? We've both lost someone. I know it's a lot harder on you, but we need to help each other now," I say to her, leaning forward to be closer to her.

She doesn't reply, so I say I'll see myself out and tell her she can message me if she ever needs to.

She stays kneeling there for hours until her husband comes to pick her up in his arms. They cry together all night, questions swirling around their heads, the words of Javan's letters flashing through their minds. There is nothing they can do now.

STILL THREE WEEKS LATER:
A VERY IMPORTANT MEETING

Everyone meet me at Paradox in 15 mins, I type into the group chat, Javan's name still boldly standing its ground at the bottom of the screen.

Len and Jenk are both sitting on a bench waiting for me by the time I pull up into the car park. I walk over to join them and throw a spliff onto the table.

"Right. We've got a lot of shit to talk through, guys. Where do we start?" I begin.

"I think we should have a proper chat about... you know... that night," Len hesitates.

"Brilliant idea, Len. Javan was gay for you," I confess, already knowing this was going to be my first topic.

"What?" he asks, looking worried and confused.

"I found a load of notes in his drawers, one from Amsterdam, one from that night and God knows how many more. But most of them talked about how jealous he was of me and you," I explain.

Jenk shakes his head in disbelief at the drama, as he lights up the spliff.

"How do you know he fancied me and not you? You two were together in year six and we all know he never got over you. Can you blame him?" He winks at me.

"He says your name in the notes, Len. It was definitely you!" I try to convince him.

"That's crazy... so he was gay all this time?" Jenk asks.

"You'd think so, Jenkies." I raise an eyebrow at him. "Now that's out the way. Did you see the news?" I move on.

"No?" Len mumbles.

"They've drawn these sketches of what the victim might have looked like. I don't recognise him but there's something that's so familiar." I get the sketches up on my phone and show them both.

"I see what you mean. There's something about the eyes," Jenk mutters. He looks up from the sketch and looks at Len.

"They've got eyes like you," he says, nodding his head towards Len.

He looks panicked, scanning both of our faces to see if we are worried, too.

"Are these sketches of the murderer?" he shouts.

"No, Len. Calm down, it's the victim. And I'm

pretty sure you're still alive." I attempt to relieve some of his stress.

He lets out a big breath of air before sinking back onto the bench and taking the spliff out of Jenk's hand.

"So far, we don't really know anything about it," I say, as I finally sit down.

"We've not been doing enough drugs!" Jenk shouts, something that's obviously been on his mind.

"Well, we've got the Skagss gig in a couple of nights, so which drug do you want to do?" I ask.

"I can get us some ket," Jenk shrugs.

"That's dirty, but go on then," I reply. We need to find the truth.

Len decides to search the internet for more information on the murder, and to our surprise we actually find a report that we haven't seen before.

"Says here that the murder weapon was a rock," he reads out to us.

"What the fuck? How did we not hear this?" Jenk questions.

"No idea... We were in a world of our own, though, I doubt we would have heard anything."

"Do you reckon we can go and have a look?" Len asks and darts his glance back and forth between me and Jenk.

After about five seconds, the answer we arrive at is 'yes'. We take the slightly longer walk to the crime scene from the other bench and approach the roll of police tape hanging around a group of trees. It's dark and we can't see much apart from the yellow tape surrounding it. Jenk turns his phone torch on and shines it at the ground in front of us.

For a split second, in the flash of the light, I see Gaz rushing towards me through the police tape with his arms outstretched and an angry look on his face. My eyes blink rapidly as if I have epilepsy and I stumble backwards. Suddenly, I begin to cry, without even thinking about it.

"Why are you crying, baby?" Len comes over to comfort me.

But I don't know why, so I don't say anything.

I wipe my tears and tell him that I'm okay. I walk back over to the crime scene and have a look around. The ground has been cleared of everything so there's not much to look at. I walk around a little bit, I search the floor for any clues, making sure to check every patch of dirt. Behind a bush, I see some faint lines across the soil. The bushes surrounding them keeps them covered from anybody who didn't know they were there. It must be from when I passed out after my wild wee. How embarrassing.

4 WEEKS LATER:

FUCKING WELL KETTY!

I drive to Jenk's house and wait for him outside. He appears in the porch, his head almost invisible behind the top of the door. He dances out, holding two bottles of orange liquid in his outstretched limbs. He gets in and shows off his bottles.

"Vodka orange, waheyhey," he sings.

I laugh at him and put the car in first gear. I can tell that Jenkies is buzzing for this gig since he hasn't stopped singing along to the songs playing in my car since we left his house, and we're now pulling up outside Len's. He rushes out of the front door and fumbles into the car with a frown on his face.

"What's up with you?" I ask him.

"Nothing," he quips.

"Do you want one of these, Len?" Jenk shouts, pushing one of the bottles right into Len's face.

"Nah, I'm alright," he sulks.

We decide to ignore it and carry on as normal. We can usually guide him into a better mood. Jenk is still singing, dancing and swinging his bottles around in the car on the way to the station, which is making Len crack a feeble smile at last. Just as I'm pulling into the car park, Jenk belts out a line of the lyrics to the song that's playing and holds up his bottle in relation to the words, but immediately regrets it.

"*START MIXING ALL OUR DRINKS A LIL' STRONGER!* I feel sick."

We laugh at him, because there's nothing more we can do now, we're here.

By the time the train arrives, Jenk is looking worse for wear. Len takes a seat at the end of the carriage whilst me and Jenk stand near him in the entrance of the train. I watch Jenk slowly swaying with the motion of the train, his eyes almost shutting and then springing back open. He leans forward to get closer to Len, who flinches, thinking he's going to throw up on him.

"Can I sit there?" he mumbles to him. So, Len gets up and comes to stand with me.

We both watch over him, laughing quietly to ourselves as he's slumped in the seat with his head between his knees. Once we get to Manchester, we're out on the hunt looking for a sheltered place to smoke. In short notice, we come across an empty church car park. I spark up as Len and Jenk have a slash against the church wall, Jenkies being pretty much horizontal as he tries not to piss on his trainers. We only pass around the spliff once before the church's security guy walks up to us and tells us to leave. Which we do, obviously. But only to the opposite side of the road where the park is. We sit on a group of rocks situated next to a scatter of headstones that seem to belong to horses.

"Right then, shall we smoke this, do a bomb and then smoke another one?" Len asks.

Jenk shrugs, with a sad face. I look at Len and he's smirking so I just take it as a joke.

We finish the spliff and begin to create our bombs. I hold the cig paper as Jenk scoops out a couple of keys from the bag and tips them in. On the third one, however, he puts about six keys into the paper.

"That one's for me." He nods with a raised eyebrow.

I don't question it; he can do what he wants. We swallow it and spark another spliff since it takes longer to kick in if taken this way.

"I feel sick," Jenk says again as he puts the spliff in his mouth and lights it.

"What you smoking that for then?" I laugh.

"Yolo." He shrugs and laughs, obviously unable to think of any other response.

After we've smoked, we get up and walk to a cash point so Jenkies can get some money out.

Me and Len stand at the side as Jenk taps on the keys of the ATM. Out of nowhere, a homeless man appears and politely asks Jenk for some money.

"I haven't got any," he says, as he pulls the ten pound note out of the machine and slides it into his wallet.

"Come on, I need a place to stay," the man begs.

"Nah, mate. Sorry," Jenk replies and begins to walk towards us.

"YOU FAGGOT!" the homeless man shouts at the back of Jenk's head.

Me and Len start shouting and jeering as we can't help but laugh at the situation.

We get to the venue, and hand our tickets over to security to check. Me and Len get into the same line and our tickets are given the slightest rips in the top corner, perfect to display on the wall once we get home. Jenkies' ticket, however, is pretty much ripped in half and hanging by a thread. He holds it up to show us,

"What the fuck!" The ticket dangles down onto his hand.

Nothing seems to be going right for our Jenkies tonight, but it makes us laugh, so we carry on.

As the support act is on, Jenk and Len go for yet another wee and so I'm left standing there, jigging to the music on my own. I turn around and a small, mousy-looking girl runs up to my face and shouts,

"I'm fucking well Ketty!" as she thrusts her gun fingers back and forth into my face as well.

I stand there looking at her expressionlessly at first, until I recognise her. Even then, all I do is raise my eyebrows and give a slight smile before turning away and going to meet Len and Jenk who have just reappeared through the doors.

"Is that McKetty over there?" Len asks, nodding towards her.

"Unfortunately." I roll my eyes.

We see that she has spotted us again and so we sneak off into the nearby smoking area. It's quiet and reasonably small, and there's only two other people there.

I say hi to them and we sit on the bench that they're stood in front of. We light a cig and start chatting, then Jenk says; "I feel sick" again. Shortly followed by, "I'm gonna be sick."

He rushes off to the back of the smoking area and starts throwing up in an empty plant pot.

The other two people are flinching and wincing at the sound of Jenk's vom spilling out onto the floor.

"Sorry about this, he's a whitey boy," I apologise to them.

"Nah, it's alright, we've all been there," they reply, before swiftly finishing up their cigs and walking back inside the venue.

"How embarrassing," Len leans into me and says.

"Don't be tight, he can't help it." I stick up for Jenkies and give Len a quick back hand to the arm.

The crowd roars as Skagss waltz onto the stage, beer cans in hand.

"Jenk, they're on," I shout over to him.

He wipes his mouth and follows us in through the doors.

The whole crowd is a mosh pit as the first few songs are played. I'm repeatedly getting pushed into the sharp marble bar behind me, but I'm much more interested in watching the band play. Slowly but firmly, I'm being pushed further and further towards the smoking area door again. Thinking it's just the motion from the mosh pit, I go along with it. It's not until I turn my head that I see Jenkies slugging behind me, his arms stretched out in front of him, sliding over the bar. I step out of the way and he slips straight out of the door. I don't go out to check on him, but I keep my eyes on the door until I see him reappear for his favourite song. He jumps around in the mosh pit, pushing everyone around until the song ends, then he runs back out though the door. He manages to stay for most of the gig, even buying a T-shirt before we leave.

We get back onto the train and Jenk doesn't say much. Me and Len have a quiet chat together as we keep our eye on him, like parents watching over a sleeping baby.

We pull into our station and Jenk seems to be in a

rush to get off, so we make it quick. Before the train even has chance to pull out from the platform, Jenkies is throwing up again. This time it's like water, he has nothing more to give. Everybody on the train sits and watches him, front row, bent over on the platform as the clear liquid soon becomes crimson red, floating away in a stream of rainwater into a small storm drain.

"I'll go and bring the car round!" Half being helpful and half just wanting not to witness the scene unfolding in front of me.

When I finally pull up in front of the train station, Jenk has a fragile arm bent around Len's neck as Len drags him off the platform and out of the station. He throws him into the back seat of the car and gets in the front.

"I'm starving..." Len sighs. "Shall we go Maccies?"

I offer no reply except for an exaggerated head tilt towards Jenkies, slumped down in the corner of the back seat.

"You don't want to go Maccies, do you?" I ask him.

"You can go," he mumbles, lifting his head slightly as he speaks.

"Come on then. We'll be quick."

I pull up in a space in the empty car park next to Maccies and we leave Jenkies to sleep in the passenger's side seat, window slightly cracked, in case he needs to throw up again.

"I hope you're all right, but if you throw up in my car, I'm never giving you a lift again," I warn him, to which he groans and gives one feeble nod of his head.

We order and sit at a table that we can see the car from, just in case Jenkies needs help. I text him to ask if he wants anything, but he says he's okay. We eat one of the best Maccies I've ever had and head back to the car. Once close enough, I decide to play a little prank on Jenkies and lock the doors. His eyes slam open and his head spins around on his neck, but when he sees us, he instantly calms down and I unlock the doors.

The drive home consists of silence and trying not to wake up Jenkies, as he's better off asleep.

I pull up outside his house and gently tap him.

"You're home," I whisper.

He slowly cracks open his eyes and fumbles for the door handle.

"Goodnight, mate, text us in the morning, let us know how you're feeling," I say to him as he gets out of the car.

"Alright," he mumbles again.

"Jenkies?"

He glumly spins around to look at me.

"Finesse, never stress." I smile at him.

He forms his own feeble smile and stumbles towards his front door.

I drive to Len's house and we both fall asleep as soon as our heads hit the pillow.

Unfortunately, the same can't be said for Jenkies.

His vision blurs as he struggles up the stairs. He crashes into his bedroom and flings off his clothes, leaving them in an untidy pile on the floor. He slowly lies down on the bed. He takes a sip of water and throws it back up seconds later, leaving a puddle on his floor. He feels too grim to do anything about the mess on the floor so he turns over onto his back and tries to close his eyes. This sends him west and his eyes flutter behind their armour of skin. As he lies on his back, dazed, scared and immobile, he throws up for one last time, but, immobilised on his back, he chokes on his own vomit and dies in his bed.

5 WEEKS LATER:
JENK'S ALIVE!

It's the day of Jenk's funeral, which his dad and his sisters organised together.

I finally get to Len's house and we make our way to the crematorium together.

All Jenk's family are already there and we introduce ourselves to the people we haven't met before. In the corner of the room is a life-sized cutout of Jenkies wearing his signature bucket hat. I point it out to Len and we have a quiet chuckle together. Jenk's sister walks over to us and we give her a hug.

"How you doing?" I ask her.

"Definitely been better, but we're supposed to be celebrating his life, not mourning his death," she explains.

"Yeah, exactly. We love that cutout of him," I tell her.

"Ha-ha, yeah, that was my idea. You can have it after the ceremony if you want?" she offers.

"We'll take him everywhere with us," I assure her.

The priest enters the room and we all take our seats. Jenk's dad reads out a letter that he'd written for Jenk, his sisters doing the same, and there wasn't a dry eye in the house. It was funny seeing pictures of him as a little kid. I just could never imagine him being small, and he wasn't, all that was missing was the bucket hat to make him look exactly as he did now.

At the end of the service, we talk to his family again and his sister passes us the cardboard cutout.

"Take good care of him," she says, as she hovers his cardboard legs under my arm.

"We will." I nod and smile.

I sit him in the back of my car, where he always sat, and we drive home listening to his favourite Tenacious Toes song. Long live Jenkies.

We drive back to Len's and when we turn the corner onto the street where his house sits, we see a couple of police cars parked on the kerb. As we crawl past, we see that there is nobody in them. We walk into his house and his mum comes through the hall to greet us.

"The police want to take you both to the station

for questioning. They won't tell us what it's about, though," she explains.

We are each directed towards a different police car and reluctantly climb into the back before being chauffeured to the station.

On the way there, I lose sight of the car carrying Len and have no idea where he's been taken, but on arrival at the station I'm directed to a small, miserable room with only three metal chairs and a metal table, all bolted to the floor. A fat, balding policeman walks into the room, closes the door behind him and sits down in front of me, all whilst staring me in the eyes and not saying a word.

"So... Two of your friends have killed themselves in the space of three weeks. Got something to hide?" he grumbles, the smell of coffee lingering in the air.

"Javan was hiding the fact that he was gay, and Jenkies died by accident, thank you very much. They're my friends that you're talking about. Could you have a bit more respect, please?" I order, feeling my teeth clenching and my blood boiling.

"And I'm supposed to believe you? The girl who wrote in her initial statement, *I saw Ollie stabbing a giant banana with a top hat on.* Really...?" He raises an eyebrow.

"That's what I saw!" I start to raise my voice slightly.

"We checked up on your supposed killer, Gaz, and he has an airtight alibi, with CCTV to back it up.

How do you explain that?" he lies, raising his eyebrow even higher.

"That's what I saw," I repeat, more fed up than irritated now. "I can't explain it. I was very tired."

"Pass me your shoes," he demands.

"What?" I ask, scrunching up my face.

"We're taking your shoes as evidence."

"Is that what you think was the murder weapon?" I joke, not wanting to give up my favourite trainers.

"Are you saying that they were? Is that why you don't want to give them to me?" he asks, clearly not getting on my level of humour.

I laugh at how pathetic he's being and pass over my shoes.

"What am I supposed to wear instead?" I ask him, sitting back in the uncomfortable metal chair that digs into my spine.

"Not my problem."

He gets up from his seat, puts my shoes in a plastic evidence bag and walks out of the room. Taking one last look at me before he closes the door. Leaving me alone in the stark, depressing room again for hours before being led out and left, shoeless, to find my own way home.

6 WEEKS LATER:

BALLOON OF DOOM

After a long, draining week, I really feel like I want to let my hair down and forget about everything that's going on, just for one night. A friend, Annie, invites me to her house party not far from Len's house, so I decide to attend. I throw on an outfit that fits me the best, punching yet another hole in my belt to make it tighter. There are crowds of people already there when I turn up, way more people than can fit inside the house. I push through the groups of people in the hallway, giving them all a smile and a greeting. There are some people here that I recognise from high school and so I chat with them for a while before heading outside, where I spot my friend.

"Alright, Annie?" I put my arm around her shoulder and pull her in for a hug.

"Thanks for coming, Flic, I know you've had a lot going on," she begins, before I stop her going any further.

"I know. I kind of want to forget about it for tonight, though," I explain to her.

"This'll help." She winks and passes me a bag of dubious-looking white powder and a balloon.

I sniff two keys and hold onto the balloon.

"I'll let that kick in first," I laugh, and she nods in agreement.

After a few minutes, Annie has to rush inside to stop a pair of idiots throwing stuff around her house and so I take a little stroll through the garden. I see a couple of people I know sitting on a bench on the other side of the road and so I cut down the side of the house to get to them. I start inhaling and exhaling into my balloon as I begin to walk. Before I even make it out of the side gate, my surroundings start to slide around in my eyes. I stumble to one side but manage to catch myself and straighten up before stumbling again to the opposite side and hitting the wall, passing out and falling onto the grass.

I'm walking through Paradox, high on MD and desperate for a wee. My vision keeps flashing white, like a set of strobe lights facing directly into my eyes and everything seems hazy. As I get to a clear patch of ground I look around, and suddenly, out of nowhere, Gaz, who is crouched behind a bush, extends his legs and comes running at me with his arms outstretched, one holding a knife. I flinch and try to dodge out of the way but he runs into me, sending us both hurtling over a small bush. He gets up immediately and takes a couple of steps back to properly look at me. I look up at him from the ground and he smiles an equally dirty smile.

I come back into reality and I'm lying pretty much spread-eagled on the grass in between Annie's house and the fence, one deflated yellow balloon crumpled up next to my head. I get up and continue to walk over the road.

"Alright, Flic? Where've you been?" my mates ask me.

I smile. "I've been around. What are you doing over here?" I ask them.

"Waiting for a dealer."

It's not long before he turns up. A black, shadowy figure wrapped in a black hoodie. He walks up to us and hands over the gear and takes the money, then pulls his hood down.

"Ryan?" I frown. Surely it can't be true?

"Yeah, what you after? 10s, 20s?"

"Nah, your mum's been out looking for you for months, you know! There's a missing person report on you and everything!" I explain to him, just in case he isn't aware of his own disappearance.

"I know. I ran away, couldn't stand her being so protective."

"Me and my mates thought you were dead.

Fucking hell. This has scrambled my brains." I sit on the bench and hold my head in my hands.

They ask why we thought he was dead, and I explain the story to them. They look equally as mind-blown by the whole situation as I am. I suggest to Ryan that he should probably let his mum and dad know that he's safe, at least, and he ponders the idea.

At the end of the night, I walk over to Len's and fill him in on the Ryan revelation as he attentively listens and strokes my hair.

DECEMBER:
RISKING IT ALL FOR SOCKS

I've made it to my last month of living and, to celebrate, we've scheduled one last blow-out before I'm too weak to move. My favourite place of all time. Home to the happiest day of my life. Claimant of some of the best moments I've ever had. And champion of all things enjoyable. Amsterdam. This time I'm going with Laurie, and an old family friend we haven't seen in years, Suze.

On our first day there, we buy a gram of lemon haze, and wander around countless museums and spend hours in the zoo, getting stoned throughout, of course. Towards the end of the day, though, Suze's feet hurt from rubbing in her shoes after walking so much, and so she asks if we can nip into H&M for some socks, and we agree, but only if it's quick. We walk in and spot a lift on the ground floor,

"What floor is it?" Suze says as we step inside.

"One," Laurie says, with a mundane look.

A few more people cram into the small, unsafe-looking lift and press all of the five buttons. None of them are speaking English and so we start to joke around as the lift takes off.

"Might as well have run your hand down the buttons!" Laurie laughs.

"Ha-ha, or accidentally stand up against them!" Suze laughs, too and then goes to demonstrate.

As she leans back onto the silver walls, a loud thud echoes through the lift shaft and the red rings around the buttons all switch off. Everybody looks at each other, and people at the front press their floor number again, but the red ring doesn't appear.

"The lights aren't coming back on. I think the lift's stuck," I say to Laurie and Suze as the other 'liftees' panic in Dutch.

They get onto the emergency phone and start talking rapidly in a language that we don't understand.

Laurie and I slightly bend our knees, ready for impact, and Laurie wonders whether she should text Mum and Dad to tell them we love them.

"What's going on?" I call out to anybody who will grace me with an answer.

"The lift has stopped. But they can't locate the shop," replies a man.

"Great," I say to myself.

Thankfully, the guy on the emergency phone has a lanyard around his neck, belonging to the shop, so he knows how to deal with these sorts of things. He gets off the call about five minutes later and just props himself up against the wall.

After another ten minutes, he walks up to the door and braces himself, his hands ready to tear open the lift doors. All I can think is, *I hope we don't die.* I'm not ready to die a few weeks earlier than scheduled! The doors slowly separate and a bright white light floods in through the crack. Oh my God, this is Heaven! No. It's the ground floor of H&M.

Everybody lets out a relieved giggle and we all make our way to our designated floors via the stairs.

We get on an escalator in the middle of the first floor, since we couldn't actually find the socks that a shop assistant promised would be here. When we get about halfway up, I turn around and see a small, creepy man holding his phone at head level and pointing it right at us. Laurie notices, too and pulls a worried face at me. Great! We just survived a near death experience with a lift (that hadn't even moved) and now we're about to be trafficked! We finally find these bloody socks, swiftly pay for them, after waiting in line for fifteen minutes, and exit the building as soon as possible, glad to be back out in the fresh Amsterdam Winter air.

"At least we're away from the traffickers now," I say to Laurie, who's looking happy.

"He's got a video, it's not going to be hard to find a girl with blue hair, with a blonde girl and a brown-haired girl!" she argues.

"Oh, yeah."

We get back to our apartment quite late and so we decide to roll a spliff and then go to bed.

Me and Laurie do our usual rolling set-up; I grind the weed and put everything back into the bag while she rolls.

"Why don't you just grind all of the weed now, so you don't have to keep doing it?" Suze asks.

"Never thought of that," Laurie answers.

"Nobody else does it, though?" I wonder, but we try it anyway.

I grind the haze, but stop short once I struggle with finding the best way to transport the weed from the grinder into the snap bag.

"I'll do it," Suze offers, so I pass it all to her.

She starts by trying to pull the bag over the grinder, but it isn't wide enough. That doesn't stop her, however, and when I see her go to tip the grinder upside down in hopes that the weed will magically transport into the bag, I have to stop her myself.

"DON'T do that!" I panic.

She looks up at me through her long, thick eyelashes and laughs before passing it back over to me. A little bit of weed falls out onto her leg, which she swiftly swipes onto the floor. Laurie and I both throw our hands to our heads in devastation.

"I can't believe you've just done that." Laurie shakes her head with a dazed look on her face.

Suze just shrugs and laughs. Weed doesn't mean that much to her.

On the second day, we pick up some shrooms in the morning and pop in to a few of the alleyway coffee shops. The first one we go into looks more like a basement brothel than a coffee shop. The room is barely lit apart from small red lights and I find myself having to really concentrate on where I'm going. We walk up to the counter and the husky old man asks us what kind of weed we want.

"Something to make us laugh!" Suze suggests.

"Thiz iz what you *nid*," he says, in his fancy foreign accent.

The only place to sit is on a bench that stretches across three of the back walls, so we choose the corner.

I dodge my way in behind the table to find that I'm sitting next to a cat, which is staring up at me with big, curious, green eyes. It chassés around me for a few seconds before jumping down on to the floor and curling up next to a hunched-over man in a striped jumper who's sitting at the table next to ours.

He's rolling a spliff very aggressively on the table, so I can't help but watch. Midway through, he picks up one of his papers on the table and starts to eat it.

"He just ate the paper," I whisper hurriedly.

"What?" they both reply, very confused.

"He just put the paper in his mouth and now he's eating it."

They both turn to look at the same time, but thankfully he doesn't notice, but they see that he's still chewing something. Unbelievably, after he's finished that one, he then eats another. I decide it's best not to watch him anymore.

Someone who still chooses to watch, though, is Suze. She is sat blatantly staring at the new group of people sitting right next to us on the adjacent table.

"Going to introduce us to your new mates?" I say to her, flicking my head towards the group.

"Want to go and join them?" Laurie says, also flicking her head towards them.

We can't stop crying with laughter. The guy behind the bar shouts over to us.

"It's working good, eh?" He laughs and gives us a thumbs-up.

Indeed.

We head over to another, bigger, more iconic coffee shop to see what we can find in there. It's packed and there aren't any seats, but we go to the bar anyway and hope that by the time we've gotten a drink, there'll be some free seats.

As we stand here, I see a guy to our left who's sitting on a bar stool and he looks like he's having a hard time. Suddenly, he tips back off his perch and lands on the floor, hitting his head on a chair on the way down. A few people gather around him, me and Laurie already being next to him anyway, and watch him as he slowly comes around. His eyes squint open and he, all of a sudden, looks very scared and confused. He looks me in the eye and I try to look as friendly as possible.

"You're okay." I nod and smile at him.

"You're safe." Laurie does the same.

He still looks dazed and gets helped up by another man who'd come over to check on him. He grabs his coat from around the stool and walks out of the door, rubbing his head.

"Bit scary, that," I say to Laurie.

"Mhmm!" she agrees with wide eyes.

We spot a table becoming available on the upper floor, so we all race up the stairs and claim it as ours. Once we've finally got everything sorted, we chill out with a glass of wine and a spliff at last. Instead of feeling hyper and giggly, though, I feel contently tired and relaxed and so I sit back in my chair and people watch. A group of three teenage girls have just arrived, sipping their mocktails and dancing terribly to the remixed tunes blasting through the building. I can't help but laugh and Suze blatantly films them and laughs too, all in good humour. Eventually, they see us watching them and their smiles turn to embarrassed frowns, but it's not long before they are prancing around again to the next song.

A middle-aged couple walk past us and Suze starts a conversation with them, since Laurie and I are not very talkative in this state. The man clearly wishes he could have done this when he was younger and is a lot more open and fun compared to his wife, who looks like she'd rather be sat watching over a detention class. They sit down across from us and it's not long before Suze offers him some of her spliff, since she doesn't feel ready for our lemon haze, and he comes over, smokes a bit and has a chat with us about the drugs he tried when he was younger. His wife is still sitting down, burning holes into the back of his head. When he returns to her, they have a very heated argument and, throughout the night, they make up, argue, make up, argue again, make up again, and argue AGAIN. They say "'Bye" to us before they leave and she puts on a 'hey, I'm chill about it' smile, as if we hadn't seen her telling him off as she pointed at our table. We call it quits not long after they do, and we go back to the apartment.

We group some chairs together and bring the duvet covers from the bed so we can be extra relaxed. Suze plays her soul music on the surround sound and we switch on the colour-changing light on the floor that illuminates the small corner of the room.

We chew through a box of shrooms each.

"There's a bit left here if anyone wants it?" Suze asks, holding up a small truffle.

"Just put it on the floor with the rest of the weed," I joke, making Laurie crack up.

It takes about half an hour to kick in, by which time we've moved around the room and sat on the bed. The painting on the adjacent wall features a golden woman with big, bright red lips, wading shoulder deep through a golden sea. Seemingly out of the blue, the water begins to swish around her body and the waves begin to glide and slowly collide into each other. The small, colourful light that only lit up a small portion of the room is now flooding the entire room with its fluorescent colours.

We sit back in our circle of chairs and do some dingers. I take long, slow breaths before opening my eyes and having a look around. Like watching a vintage 3D film without the glasses, a jagged line of pink and green outlines every shape. Laurie attempts to build her dinger, picking up a balloon, a capsule and our new golden cracker, but she struggles to make sense of everything. Eventually, she puts the capsule into the cracker, and yet again, confusion washes over her. She twists the cracker, without the balloon on the end, into the palm of her hand.

"I've froze me fuckin' hand off!" she screams in a panic, holding her hand in the air by her wrist.

Suze and I crack up and reassure her that her hand is fine. Laurie finally gets her dinger and she says that everything was leaving a trail as it moved, so naturally I start waving my long arms around in front of her and she watches open-mouthed in astonishment, following every movement with her head.

We decide to do one more, but all together this time. We start puffing into our balloons when I suddenly have a thought.

"Imagine if this was helium! PAHAHA, MY NAME'S FELICITY!" I squeak.

Laurie laughs into her dinger and it's sent flying around the room. Sending us all into hysterics.

There's another painting of a woman, behind Laurie; this one is all grey apart from flaming red hair atop a geometric face. As I move my head left and right, the woman's face moves with me, as if it's a 3D sculpture on a digital display.

"Shall we smoke the rest of that?" Laurie suggests, nodding towards two halves of a spliff on the table.

"Go on then," I agree, with mushroom-fuelled confidence.

All seems fine at first, but my legs cannot stay still. Soon, nothing makes sense.

"You don't look like you're having fun," Suze

says, reasonably sober since she didn't smoke any weed.

Out of nowhere, I'm sent into a different dimension where only I exist, on a new planet full of new and curious objects, I don't recognise any of them, or know what their use is, but I look at everything in detail. How can you travel to a completely new world, without moving an inch? Drugs.

Suze gets bored with mine and Laurie's blank staring and leaves to lie down on the bed and talk to her friend on the phone. I move over to Laurie and sit with her. Not only is it cold in the room, but it's also nice to know I'm not alone in my unfamiliar world. Laurie stares at a picture of New York, coming to life with the yellow taxis zooming around on the road.

I look outside the window into the night sky and see a hole forming between the array of stars. It gets bigger and bigger until it swallows me, and spits me back out, onto an old wooden bench, covered in graffiti. Three lads are sat with me. In front is a very tall guy with shoulder-length hair and a nice bucket hat. Next to him is a sad boy, slumped on the bench, his pointy elbow almost piercing through the wood. And next to me is the most beautiful thing I've ever seen; big pearly white teeth, sparkling blue eyes and hair as soft and white as freshly fallen snow. I stand up from the bench and follow a path leading into the forest. I find a flat area and scope my surroundings. Out of the corner of my eye, I see movement and when I turn, a scary-looking man, with a face full of scars runs towards me with his arms out to grab me. I try to dodge out the way, but he sends us both hurtling over a small bush that is behind me. He grabs me by the throat and tries to choke me. I pick up a rock from next to my leg and I hit him over the side of the head with it again and again, with as much force as I can possibly conjure, before rolling over to gasp for air, and passing out there on the hard, muddy ground.

I'm shaking and sweating uncontrollably, and my eyes dart around the room as my heartbeat grows faster and faster inside my chest, as if my heart wants to escape my body and run away from the horror that I just relived. I feel like I could throw up any minute, so I stand up and announce that I'm going to join Suze on the bed. A deck of playing cards has fallen onto the floor next to us, so I bend down and pick up every card, one by one, concentrating like never before, to take my mind away from what I'm feeling and what I just saw. *Pick one up. Pick two up. Pick three up. Pick four up*, I continue in my head, until there are no cards left for me to count. I balance them gently on the table, my hands still quivering. I walk down the two creaky wooden steps that lead from the sitting area to the bedroom, and as soon as I put one foot down on the bedroom floor, all of the bad feelings disappear, and I feel like I was never in that other dimension, I never felt that pain, I never did those things.

We get to the airport the next morning, say our farewells to Suze as she flies back to London and we head to the gate for Manchester. We quickly make a visit to the very futuristic smoking area which is in the middle of one of the departure lounges. Sadly, half-way through Laurie's cig, a cleaner comes in and tells us we must leave. We take it with a pinch of salt and carry on as normal, until... enter the arguing couple from the coffee shop. Laurie takes short, quick puffs until she reaches the filter and we leg it out of there as quick as possible. Which doesn't make much of a difference, since we end up seated next to them on the plane home.

FINAL

So, there it is. That's the truth about what happened that night. Without even knowing it, I killed a man in self-defence and went on with the rest of my life none the wiser until the last minute. I say nothing to my family about my newly discovered crime as they circle me in my hospital bed. My mum is sat next to me, holding my hand, my dad on the other side. I stare at them quietly as tears stream out of their eyes.

"Don't cry. I'm happy," I manage to whisper.

Len and Laurie sit further down, both with a tight, protective grip on my legs. Len is in bits and can't stop sobbing onto my thin, white covers. I can feel the wetness sticking the sheet to my leg.

"I love you all," I say and I smile, looking around at everybody.

Literally the entire family has turned up to say goodbye. Even Jenk's cardboard cutout is stood static, smiling at me, behind the crowd of sorrowful faces.

"I'm so lucky to have spent my life with you all," I continue.

"We love you too, Flic," people whimper in chorus.

I look at them all one last time,

"Thank you."

I close my eyes, never to open them again.

Life may be short, but it's the longest thing we'll ever know.

ONE YEAR LATER

J avan's family finally make peace with their son's suicide. After reading through all of his notes, they realise he wasn't happy in this life, and he's now moved on to a better, kinder place where he's happy and free.

Jenk's family continue to live their lives but miss him eternally. They never tell anybody his true cause of death, pinning it on heart failure. His headstone stands proudly in the graveyard, the words, *Finesse, Never Stress*, plastered across the top of it. His legacy continues in the form of his cardboard cutout.

Flic passes away on the first of January 2019. When trawling through her belongings, a diary is discovered. On the first page, in big bold letters, are the words, *Gone Too Far West*. Her family fight to get the book published in order to set the record straight, but consistently broadcast her innocence in relation to the murder.

As for Len, he can't handle the loss of his two best friends and his girlfriend. He slowly begins to spiral into lunacy. Eventually, he is hospitalised in a facility called George Lee's psychiatric hospital, where doctors and investigators observe him day after day, to study his mental disorders, as well as try to elicit his version of events to confirm those of Flic, but all they get from him are fantastical stories about four pirates who witness a murder on their boat, Black Beauty, or four astronauts who witness a murder on the moon.

His case is catalogued in an upcoming book: *Len World*.

Dear reader,

We hope you enjoyed reading *Gone Too Far West*. Please take a moment to leave a review, even if it's a short one. Your opinion is important to us.

Discover more books by Isobel Wycherley at

https://www.nextchapter.pub/authors/isobel-wycherley

Want to know when one of our books is free or discounted? Join the newsletter at

http://eepurl.com/bqqB3H

Best regards,

Isobel Wycherley and the Next Chapter Team

YOU MIGHT ALSO LIKE

You might also like:
Len World by Isobel Wycherley
To read the first chapter for free, please head to:
https://www.nextchapter.pub/books/len-world

ABOUT THE AUTHOR

I was born on the 13th of September, 1999 in Warrington, England.

I wrote this, my first book, when I was eighteen, based around my experiences in the summer of 2018.

I study linguistics at Manchester Metropolitan University, I am interested in pursuing forensic linguistics and have an interest in acquisition.

I love music, it's always been a big part of my life, as well as helping me to establish a positive attitude towards anything. Films are another love of mine, which I try to reflect in my writing style, since I generally picture my stories as films playing out in my head, which helps me to imagine what I would want to see happen next, if it really were a film.

I'm very inquisitive and want to know everything about everything. I love learning and experiencing new things and I can't wait to see where that takes me, especially in my new writing career.

Gone Too Far West
ISBN: 978-4-86747-063-3
Large Print

Published by
Next Chapter
1-60-20 Minami-Otsuka
170-0005 Toshima-Ku, Tokyo
+818035793528

18th May 2021

Lightning Source UK Ltd.
Milton Keynes UK
UKHW010040291122
413021UK00003B/39